"You move a muscle and ⌐
said.

Slocum laughed harshly and sat up.

"Your gun jammed. I saved you. And then it looks like you saved me, so we're even. Thanks."

The bullet ripping through the crown of his hat sent the Stetson flying. Slocum stared at the mail clerk, who had cast aside his six-shooter in favor of a smaller pistol that had been stashed in his vest pocket. The derringer almost disappeared in the man's grip, but from the determination on the man's face, death was about to visit Slocum . . .

JAKE LOGAN

SLOCUM
AND THE
BULLET EXPRESS

JOVE BOOKS, NEW YORK

THE BERKLEY PUBLISHING GROUP
Published by the Penguin Group
Penguin Group (USA) LLC
375 Hudson Street, New York, New York 10014

USA • Canada • UK • Ireland • Australia • New Zealand • India • South Africa • China

penguin.com.

A Penguin Random House Company

SLOCUM AND THE BULLET EXPRESS

A Jove Book / published by arrangement with the author

For information, address: The Berkley Publishing Group,
a division of Penguin Group (USA) LLC,
375 Hudson Street, New York, New York 10014.

ISBN: 978-0-515-154399

PUBLISHING HISTORY
Jove mass-market edition / April 2014

PRINTED IN THE UNITED STATES OF AMERICA

10 9 8 7 6 5 4 3 2 1

Cover illustration by Sergio Giovine.

1

Being so close to the six-by-nine-foot iron cage where San Diego kept its prisoners made John Slocum edgy. He touched the ebony-handled Colt Navy slung in a cross-draw holster at his left hip and considered his chances. The brick courthouse was filled with men sporting battered tin badges and looking even more nervous than he was. He couldn't keep himself from staring at a small section of the wall near the entrance where a dozen brittle-edged, yellowed wanted posters had been nailed to a board. Some of the pictures might have carried his likeness. Slocum had done enough in his day to deserve a place in this rogues' gallery, but none was his that he saw.

For that, he heaved a sigh of relief because after the deadly gunplay north of town a week back, there could have been. He forced himself not to react when a clerk called his name and impatiently gestured for him to come forward. Leaving the tight knot of men that had been rounded up, Slocum went to the desk, where the mousy clerk shuffled through stacks of ink-splotched papers.

"Name?"

"I told the deputy what I saw."

The clerk looked up. His eyes didn't quite focus. Slocum stepped back a half pace to make it even harder for the near-sighted man to ever identify him. If he hadn't had his horse shot out from under him, he would have left town long ago. If he hadn't been stone broke, he would have left. And if he—

"Do you want to spend some time in the cell?" The clerk jerked his thumb over his shoulder in the direction of the iron cage ominously empty at the rear of the building. "I can get a judge to sentence you for contempt of court just like that." He snapped his fingers.

The sharp pop made many of those rounded up with Slocum reach for their six-shooters. This caused the keyed-up deputies in the courthouse to go for their pistols. After a tense moment, everyone took their hands off their six-shooters.

The clerk never noticed. He squinted, trying to bring Slocum into focus. He impatiently motioned for Slocum to step closer to the desk. Slocum stood his ground.

"I saw the man with the red bandanna throw down and fire on the man sitting in the chair."

"Did the seated man go for a gun?"

"I didn't see that he had a six-gun," Slocum said.

The saloon across the town plaza had been crowded because of the nickel whiskey being offered. A new shipment had arrived and the barkeep claimed he didn't have room to store it before it got stolen, so he wanted to sell off fifty gallons of prime Kentucky whiskey—not trade whiskey, by any means—as fast as he could. The discount had pulled in thirsty men from all over San Diego along with their desire to be first in line.

"So Mr. Goodwin wasn't armed?"

"If he was the man in the chair, I didn't see him with a gun." Slocum wondered at the uproar over one man's death. He shouldn't have but he asked, "Who was he? The dead man?"

The clerk dipped his pen, scratched a few jagged lines on his report, then looked up.

"You aren't a local? Harry Goodwin is the son of the owner of Far Orient Shipping."

"A big business?"

"None bigger. If Far Orient pulled out of San Diego and went north to Frisco, like Old Man Goodwin's been threatening to do, San Diego would be hurt worse than in the fire back in '72. That only destroyed buildings and burnt up some folks who weren't quick enough to get away. This would kill jobs, and most all of the goods that come through here would disappear. The S&P Railroad terminus here would get moved up to Frisco, more 'n likely, and not even the Mormons would want to come back to help build. Now, did you see the son of a bitch shoot Mr. Goodwin?"

Before Slocum could say a word, a bull-throated roar came from the courthouse door.

"He's here. I got people to say he's here and I want him!"

Slocum saw a mountain of bone and gristle and pure mean filling the doorway. The man wore filthy buckskins, bandoliers slung in an X across his massive chest, and pistols at either hip. A fiery red beard shot with gray or maybe debris from his last meal hung down a full foot from his chin. His florid face almost vanished in a forest of beard, bushy eyebrows, and wild hair that hung down to his broad shoulders. He shuffled forward, moving more like a bear than a man. But Slocum knew a bear could outrun a racehorse. Such power and speed could be locked within this man because of the way he shifted his weight lightly from one foot to the other as he moved. Moccasins whispered on the polished wood floor as he pushed his way into the crowded and suddenly silent lobby.

"I want him! I'm Big Joe Joseph and I got a warrant for him. I'm gonna collect my hunnerd dollars! He's mine and I'll strangle any man what says different!"

The deputies who had herded everyone into the courthouse to give statements turned to the huge man. One stepped up, holding his rifle at port arms and thinking he could back off the bounty hunter. The deputy went flying with a single backhanded swipe.

"There's the varmint what held up the San Dismas bank 'n' kilt three decent citizens."

Eyes as green as the ocean eyes fixed on Slocum. Big Joe's hands closed into fists the size of quart jars. He gripped down so hard the crunching noise again silenced the growing murmur in the courthouse. Moving as light as a feather, Big Joe came straight for Slocum.

Killing the man would be declared self-defense. With so many lawmen in the room, he'd have good witnesses—but one of them was bound to ask the unwanted question of what the bounty hunter meant about a bank robbery. That hadn't been anything to lay at Slocum's feet, not legitimately. He had been an innocent bystander, just as he had been outside the saloon when that shooting took place, when the robbers had left the bank with their guns blazing. Two customers and a bank teller had ended up bleeding on the lobby floor. As the robbers left, two more had been injured. Slocum had drawn and fired at one of the bank robbers thinking of gunning him down, and that had been a mistake.

He was left with a fired six-gun in his hand and the robbers beating a quick retreat when the marshal had shown up. In the confusion Slocum had been the only one identified. He had mounted and galloped off until a deputy shot the horse from under him. Slocum hadn't even fired back, creeping from the dead horse to a ditch and eventual escape thirty miles south to San Diego.

His luck hadn't gotten any better here.

"We got law here in San Diego," the clerk said, squinting hard. "What's the commotion about?"

"Him," Big Joe roared. "I want him!"

The bounty hunter lurched forward and grabbed for Slocum. If those massive arms had closed around him, Slocum knew the bear hug would have crushed the breath from his lungs. More likely, a broken spine would be the sorry result.

He ducked, but Big Joe Joseph spun as gracefully as any dance hall girl performing "Hell's Gallop" onstage.

Slocum moved slower and with less agility, but sliding across the desk and shoving the clerk forward bought him a few seconds to escape. The clerk doubled over, gasped out, and croaked a warning to the assembled deputies. The sight of the clerk in distress and the bounty hunter swinging his mighty fists in wide circles above his head brought a rush to save him. A half-dozen deputies grabbed at Big Joe's greasy buckskins. Some fringe pulled off. Others missed entirely and ended up in a pile on the floor.

One smart deputy swung his rifle and caught the bounty hunter behind the knees. No matter how strong Big Joe was, withstanding such an attack wasn't humanly possible. He yelped and threw his arms up in the air as he toppled backward onto the floor. The deputies already in a pile swarmed to pin him down. Slocum saw a couple men tossed up into the air. Others used the butts of their rifles to crash down on Big Joe's head. One stock bounced off as if it had hit solid iron. Then Slocum finally got through the crowd of people between him and the back door. He popped outside and hesitated at the sight of the iron cage.

If he ended up inside, he was a goner. He had no way to prove he hadn't taken any part in the San Dismas bank robbery. If Big Joe was on his trail shouting about a reward, the wanted poster said "Dead or Alive" at the bottom. From the look of him, the bounty hunter wasn't the sort to worry over much about the "Alive" part.

Slocum ran a few yards, realized he was attracting attention from people going about their business in the San Diego plaza, and slowed to a walk. He pulled down his hat to protect his face from the sun—and recognition. Not realizing it, he had headed for the harbor. Veering away, he walked south to a marketplace and lost himself in the crowd.

Tiring, Slocum found a spot in the shade and sank down, the building's adobe wall cool against his back. He slid his hat down even more on his forehead and peered out from under the brim to be certain no one came for him. For the first time since early morning and the hubbub outside the saloon, he had a chance to think. He had sought the cheap whiskey like so many others. The crowd pressing into the cantina provided him anonymity, and he had a nickel in his pocket for a shot of the prime tarantula juice. It never occurred to him a prominent citizen's son would be killed and he, along with the rest of the crowd, would be herded to the courthouse to give evidence against the killer.

Whoever had shot the Goodwin scion might also have some standing in the community. If so, that would explode into an out-of-control trial with each side blaming the other for the killing. Provocation, self-defense, business dealings, the very financial health of the city added fuel to the fire. Slocum wanted no part of it, though he started to wonder if running solved anything. How he could have proven his innocence in the San Dismas bank robbery was a poser. Bringing in the real outlaws would have helped, but going after them would have put him on the same trail and given a marshal the excuse that he was only left behind, that he had been one of the murderous gang. With his horse shot from under him, tracking the bank robbers turned into an impossible task.

Running didn't set well with him, but Big Joe Joseph on his trail meant other bounty hunters knew of the reward. He could take care of the giant, given the time and proper spot for an ambush. Slocum had dealt with meaner men in his day, and putting a slug between the man's close-set eyes would come easily. Killing someone who didn't need it if he got out of San Diego suited Slocum better than facing off with Big Joe in a bare knuckles fight.

He knew better than to hang around the docks. Shanghaiers worked all the ports along the Pacific coast. Being on a China clipper for two years when he felt better astride a horse was something he could forgo. Short of stealing a horse, though, he needed to get away fast and he had no idea how to do that. The decision came when he heard a distant train whistle. He looked up and studied everyone around him. Nobody paid him any attention. Rested, Slocum got to his feet and headed toward the freight train yards. New whistle blasts kept him moving until he reached a broad street where heavily laden wagons rolled toward a loading dock.

Slipping into a doorway, he watched and waited. A half-dozen trains were at the depot. Two of them loaded merchandise that had been shipped from halfway around the world and brought from the seagoing freighters, maybe those owned by the dead man's father. Three others had crews bustling about them, shouting and carrying on as they repaired broken rods and hammered on split boilers. The freight trains afforded him the best chance of getting out of town. Since it mattered less where he went than ending up in a cozy destination, he picked the train closest to the depot and made his way to it.

He had never ridden the rails by crawling up under a freight car and lying on the support rods dangling below the floor. More than once he had listened to a drunk's story of how dangerous it was. The story always ended with some daring escape from calamity. What Slocum got from the stories was that men traveled this way and did so often enough that the tall tales were likely only half true, if that.

The freight car he had chosen vibrated as a side door creaked along rusted rails and then slammed hard. The soft crunch followed by a click told him the door had been sealed using a lead slug with a wire run through it. Pliers clamped the lead disk down around the wire and pressed the company seal into the metal for surety. Anyone opening the door had to cut it off. Slocum listened for the crew to leave before slipping under the car and examining the rods.

Slocum wasn't fat but fitting between the freight car's floor and the spiderweb of rusted metal shafts would be tight. The slightest bump or turn as the train barreled along would crush him. He gripped one rod and exerted as much pressure on it as he could. The metal barely bent. Lying on his back, he grabbed the rod with both hands and put his feet against the freight car floor. Cinders cut into his back and made him wince as he pushed with his legs and pulled with his arms.

The rod began to bend slightly. He applied more pressure, grunting with the exertion. Rapidly approaching footsteps caused him to cease his effort and stretch back, cinders and railroad ties cutting into his back. From this vantage he saw rapidly scissoring legs coming toward him. He reached over for his six-shooter when the man stopped not five feet away. If he looked under the car, he had to see Slocum.

"Gunther! Where you at, you lazy Kraut? Gunther!"

"I'm over here, you drunken Mick. You see him or did you leave your glasses at the whorehouse again?"

Slocum jerked around. A new set of legs came up on the other side of the train. He was trapped between the German and the Irish railroad detectives. His heart hammered away. Railroad detectives had the reputation of leaving bodies behind rather than running off trespassers or turning them over to the local law.

"Might be that four-eyed clerk didn't see anyone at all," Gunther said.

Both detectives walked to the far end of the car. One crossed to join the other.

"Where do you think he went?"

"This car's all locked down. If'n he's inside, he ain't leavin'. I say we check closer to the caboose. If nobody's there, hell, we got to search each car."

"Ought to make McIlheny come with us."

"Ought to make him get new eyeglasses."

The two railroad detectives moved away, letting Slocum slip out on the far side of the train. He brushed himself off to appear less like he was trying to steal a ride and more like he belonged in a passenger car. The train on the next track had eight passenger cars linked behind it. The plumes of steam coming from the smokestack and the way the engineer and fireman cursed each other warned him the train was about to pull out. It wouldn't serve him to sneak into a passenger car. The conductor would find him right away. Without a ticket, he would be tossed off immediately and not be any better off than he was now.

Going down the line of cars, he came to a mail car. A clerk paced back and forth just inside the open door, occasionally looking at a huge black steel safe mounted in the center of the floor. To open that would require a dozen sticks of dynamite, but Slocum's intentions were to steal a ride, not the U.S. mail or whatever else might be in the safe.

The locomotive quivered and belched, then spat a ten-foot-long tongue of orange flame mixed with cinders before settling down to white steam pouring from the smokestack. The cars behind the tender clanked and pulled together as the engine slowly gathered speed. Slocum didn't care where the train was headed as long as it was away from San Diego. He jumped up on the coupling between the mail car and the passenger car in front of it.

When a black face appeared at the dirty window looking out between cars, Slocum dropped down low. The conductor didn't see him. He hung on as the train rattled through the yard and found the proper switch. They headed east. Slocum settled down on the small platform at the rear of the passenger car and braced his legs against the mail car. The city flashed past and soon the train entered the countryside, cooler here away from the adobes and horses.

Barely had he time to appreciate the twilight-cloaked world when the engineer threw on the brakes. Even as far back in the train as Slocum was, he smelled the acrid odor of burning steel. He was tossed about and grabbed a railing, hanging on to keep from being thrown off. The train hadn't gone more than a dozen miles outside town.

Two riders trained rifles on the engineer and the fireman. He had been so wrapped up in his own trouble that it hadn't occurred to him before this instant that these weren't deputies out to arrest him. They were outlaws robbing the train.

He had to admire their balls. They held up the train within miles of town. If they had let the train steam out into the desert and robbed it there, pursuit by the law would be days in coming. Their getaway was assured by the miles of emptiness and the time it'd take for the train to reach a telegraph station if they damaged the locomotive.

He slipped back, moving slowly to avoid drawing attention to himself. He eased up on the platform and peered through the dirty window into the car. Another robber held the passengers at gunpoint. The conductor went from passenger to passenger, collecting their valuables. From the glimpse Slocum had of the man's dusky face, he was about to explode in anger. Forcing the conductor to take part in the robbery was an affront not to be borne. As if he could read the man's mind, Slocum knew this was *his* train, *his* passengers, and this was a perversion of *his* duty.

Seven men. Four behind, two with the engineer, and one in this car. Slocum doubted there were any others, though he couldn't be sure. The loot taken from the passengers had to be lagniappe for the robbers. What they really wanted rested inside the big black safe in the mail car.

Slocum let the conductor see him. The man's face was contorted into fury. For an instant Slocum thought he would blurt out an angry word to the robber about yet another outlaw on the train. On *his* train. Something settled the conductor's choler as he realized Slocum intended to stop the robbery, not abet it. He stood up straight, his bulk filling the aisle and blocking the robber's view of the rear door.

"Why you doin' this?" The conductor raised his voice as Slocum opened the door. It squeaked. "You outta know Mistah Burlison's gonna be furious mad at this. He don't like the Yuma Bullet missin' its schedule. We is the best damned train fer adherin' to our timetable of any S&P train."

"Shut up," the robber called. "You keep takin' them wallets and watches. Hurry up or I'll shoot a passenger." He bent over and ran the barrel of his pistol along an old woman's cheek. "I might just start with this crone since nobody'd miss her."

Slocum moved fast, duck-walking through the door and closing it behind. The conductor shifted around, turning so Slocum had a clear shot at the robber. He hesitated with the outlaw's barrel resting alongside the woman's face. Something alerted the robber. He stood straighter and instinctively brought his six-shooter around. Slocum fired. The first round caught the outlaw in the belly. The loud *whang!* told the story. The slug had hit a big belt buckle. The second shot hit a few inches higher and gave the man a new belly button.

Staggering from the first impact, he folded over and dropped to the floor as the second bullet drove through his gut. Slocum pushed past the conductor and waited to see if a third round was necessary. The outlaw made pitiful animal sounds and thrashed about weakly. With a quick grab, Slocum took the outlaw's fallen six-gun and slid it into his belt.

"Keep the passengers in the car. There're two robbers with the engineer and four trying to break into the mail car."

"You gonna whup all of 'em?" the conductor asked. "All by yo' lonesome?"

Slocum hadn't thought it through. He smiled crookedly and only nodded. Without a decent plan and the outlaws alerted to trouble by the two gunshots, he would be walking into a buzzing hornet's nest. The irony of it all didn't escape him that this was the third time in two days he had found himself mixed up in a crime not of his doing. The bank robbery and killing of three men had brought the bounty hunter down on him. For all he knew, the San Diego marshal had a posse after him for the unpleasantness outside the saloon.

"Kill them all," he heard as he went out the car door

nearer the engine. He looked over his shoulder. The old woman the robber had threatened looked fierce enough to take on the robbers by herself. Slocum almost handed over the captured six-shooter to let her do it herself. From her determined expression, she would try.

He touched the brim of his hat and ducked onto the platform between cars. The passengers in the forward car milled about, not sure what was happening. One tried to open the door when he saw Slocum.

"What's going on? I demand to know!"

With a savage kick that sent the man reeling back into the car, Slocum kept moving. He dropped to the ground in a crouch and saw the four dark figures back at the mail car. They still banged on the side demanding to be let in.

Lack of a plan gnawed at him now. The two outlaws holding the engineer prisoner presented an easier target. Take them out and the train could build steam and pull away, forcing the four left behind to once more overtake the train. When they did, Slocum could shoot them from the saddle one by one. Only a small detail made him turn away from the locomotive and to the four. The engineer had stopped for a reason. If something had been dropped on the tracks, plowing forward might be impossible without derailing the train.

Which way to attack decided itself when one of the four spotted Slocum. A bullet sailed high and wide over his head. Slocum didn't return fire. He had too few rounds to waste any of them in the darkness. Hitting a man on a nervous horse was a hard shot at the best of times. Instead, Slocum shot at the man on the ground hammering away at the mail car door. The slug ripped away part of the wood and sent splinters into the outlaw's face, causing him to recoil. The robber triggered a round that tore away more wood, but this struck higher on the car. In reaction, the outlaws' horses all reared, giving Slocum a few seconds to rush forward.

He fired until his Colt came up empty. The shots hit

nothing. He grabbed for the gun tucked into his belt and fired off a single round. This found a mounted outlaw, more by luck than skill.

"He shot me. Damnation, he shot me!" The train robber spun about on his horse and fell when the animal reared. The man hit the ground hard, moaned, and sank down onto his belly.

Slocum doubted the man was dead, but he wasn't in the fight any longer.

Letting loose a rebel yell, Slocum closed the distance and fired twice more. Three shots. How many rounds had the outlaw already fired? The number of rounds he had left turned into the least of his worries. The three remaining outlaws fired at him now, their shots coming nearer as he closed the distance between them.

The one who had banged away on the door fired at him. Slocum heard the slug whistle past and then he tackled the man, wrestling him to the ground. The outlaw got in a lucky punch and stunned Slocum. Then he kicked him in the shoulder. Slocum's left arm turned numb, but he clung to the captured six-shooter in his right hand. Bringing it up onto target proved harder than he'd expected as another heavy blow stunned him. Driven to his knees, Slocum watched the world through pain and darkness.

The night blasted apart as a yellow tongue of flame lashed in his direction—but the bullet found his attacker, not him. Slocum blinked away the dazzle and saw the mail clerk holding a six-gun. He had chosen the best possible time to join the fight. He fired twice more and then the six-shooter jammed.

Slocum swallowed the pain and used both hands to bring up the pistol. He emptied it at the other mounted robber. His vision refused to give him a true picture of what happened, but in his gut he knew he had missed. Then he grunted in pain as strong arms circled his body, pinning his arms to his side. The pistol fell to the ground as he fought.

As quickly as he had been immobilized, he found himself staggering away free. Slocum lost his balance and hit the ground. He rolled over, ready to keep fighting but the outlaw had disappeared.

"You move a muscle and you're a dead man," the mail clerk said.

Slocum laughed harshly and sat up.

"Your gun jammed. I saved you. And then it looks like you saved me, so we're even. Thanks."

The bullet ripping through the crown of his hat sent the Stetson flying. Slocum stared at the mail clerk, who had cast aside his six-shooter in favor of a smaller pistol that had been stashed in his vest pocket. The derringer almost disappeared in the man's grip, but from the determination on the man's face, death was about to visit Slocum.

The engineer had reversed the driving rods and pushed the Yuma Bullet backward along the track all the way to the depot. Slocum sat in the mail car, hands tied and fuming at the injustice of it all. He'd expected better than for the clerk to pull a derringer on him after he saved the man from the robbers. As the train rattled and lurched along the tracks, Slocum found it impossible not to stare at the huge safe. He finally asked.

"What's in it?"

"The safe? You tried to rob the train and you don't know?" The clerk snorted, then wiped his nose on his sleeve. "That's rich. You held up the train and have no idea what you're tryin' to steal."

"I stopped the robbery. I'm not one of that gang." Slocum lifted his chin and pointed, Navajo style, at the two bodies stacked in the far corner of the car. One had tried to rob the passengers. The other had caught Slocum's bullet and hadn't gotten far enough away before he leaked too much blood.

"You had a falling-out with your partners," the clerk said.

"Is that the way the conductor saw it?"

"You leave Jefferson outta this. He's a good man but don't expect him to lie for you."

Slocum only wanted him to tell the truth. Better to be branded as trying to ride the train without a ticket than robbing it. He started to speak but a sudden lurch sent him flopping about on the floor. He skidded a few feet and fetched up hard against the wall. Shaking off the impact, he forced himself to sit upright. The clerk's pistol had never wavered.

"We're back," the clerk said. "You're in for a world of trouble now."

"You have no idea," Slocum said glumly.

The clerk pulled him to his feet and shoved him out the door. Slocum got his feet under him a split second before he fell. Landing heavily, he staggered a couple paces. The two railroad bulls stood in front of him. Both looked as he expected, if the Irishman had the red hair and the German was so blond his hair looked white in the gaslight from the depot.

"He's all yours, boys."

"Go to hell," Gunther said. He took Slocum's left arm and the Irishman the right so they could give him the bum's rush.

For a moment Slocum thought they'd take him to the depot, where the law would gladly arrest a man with offenses piled a yard high. Adding train robbing to the list seemed almost an afterthought. But the two railroad detectives steered Slocum away and toward a lighted Pullman car sitting all by itself on a siding. Even in the faint light from the railroad yard, Slocum saw this was a special car. Gilt edging and fancy lettering on the side warned him he was being taken to the head man of the railroad. Or at least the man in charge of the San Diego depot.

"Up you go," Gunther said. They heaved and Slocum sailed through the air to crash against the rear door.

The door opened and spilled him to the floor. He squinted against the bright light. All he could see were boots so

highly polished they reflected the car's gaslights as bright
as the sun.

"What are you doing down there, man? Get up! Get up,
I say!"

Slocum pushed to hands and knees. Standing with his
hands bound tightly was harder than he'd expected. His fingers had turned into bloated white sausages, and his arms
tingled from lack of circulation all the way to his shoulders.

"Why's he trussed up like that? Cut the ropes. Now!"

Gunther and his partner yanked Slocum to his feet. The
soft snick of a knife leaving its sheath ended with the Irish
detective slicing through the ropes. Slocum almost cried out
in pain as circulation rushed back into his hands.

"You two reprobates, out! Get out!"

"Yes, sir, Mr. Burlison," Gunther said. The two hastily
left, closing the Pullman door behind them.

Slocum felt as if he had been delivered to paradise. The
furnishings in the Pullman were as sumptuous as anything
he had seen at San Francisco's Union Club. Red velvet–
covered sofas reminding him of surplus from a Denver
whorehouse lined either wall. A fainting couch that looked
both fragile and expensive had been pushed to one side to
make room for a huge cherrywood desk littered with papers.
Chairs and tables made getting from one end of the car to
the other an obstacle course.

Sitting on the tables were small marble statues, some of
nudes, others of animals and mythical creatures. One had
been studded with enough diamonds to keep Slocum in
whiskey and women for a year. The way the gems sparkled
made him squint.

Wherever a bare section of wall showed itself, an oil
painting had been hung. Mostly the walls were glass, giving
a fine look out over the countryside as the lavish car was
dragged along S&P tracks.

Slocum finally finished his inventory of the richness and
saw the conductor standing in one corner, arms crossed over

his broad chest. The man's brown eyes fixed unwaveringly on Slocum. If he had blinked, it would have spoiled the impression that he was an ebony statute among the rest of the artwork.

"Mr. Jefferson, good to see you again," Slocum said. To his surprise, the conductor produced a huge grin that revealed teeth as shining white as the diamonds were brilliant.

"You, too, suh."

"Ahem." The man who so easily ordered the railroad bulls around stepped forward to block Slocum's line of sight. "You two know each other. Allow me to introduce myself. I am Morgan Burlison, vice president of the S&P Railroad, in charge of California operations."

"Only foah the moment," Jefferson said. "Mistah Burlison heah is the new head of the entire line in Texas."

"That a promotion?" Slocum rubbed his wrists until he could flex his hands again.

"Quite so, yes," Burlison said. "I will oversee all the rail lines from the Mississippi to the West Coast whereas now I am only in charge of the California system."

Slocum considered how difficult it would be to knock down Burlison and use him as a shield to get away. His two bully boys prowled about outside the car. Slocum saw the Irishman's red hair bobbing up and down as he paced from one end to the other. The shorter German probably guarded the other side of the car. But with a quick spring, he thought Burlison might be easy prey.

The man's vest bulged outward over his substantial belly. The pasty skin and hands lacking calluses spoke of long hours out of the sun doing bureaucratic work, not laying rail or driving spikes. Still, Slocum had seen big men with guts like that who proved stronger than they looked. Whatever he did had to be over fast. Jefferson was a big man, too, and carried far less fat than his boss. He was older but a man who had spent most of his life doing hard labor.

Whatever he did, he had to keep Burlison alive to order

the railroad detectives away. Kill the railroad official and nothing held Gunther and his partner in check.

"Forgive my terrible manners. Please, sir, sit." Burlison indicated one of the velvet sofas. Slocum started to brush off his jeans to keep the dirt off the fancy couch, then decided the hell with it.

He dropped heavily, a small cloud of dust rising around him. For his part, Burlison paid no heed.

"What's his name? Mr. Jefferson?"

"Nevah got it, suh. I was too busy with the passengers."

"So, Mr. . . ." Burlison let the question hang in the air.

"John Slocum." As tempting as it was to give a summer name, they had him fair and square. It wouldn't take but a few minutes for the San Dismas marshal to identify him. For all he knew, the bounty hunter's warrant carried his name already.

"From all Mr. Jefferson has said, and he is not a man to exaggerate, you saved not only his life but that of at least one passenger. Thank you."

Slocum held up his raw wrists. Blood oozed onto his shirt cuff from where the mail clerk had so savagely tied him up.

"You have a strange way of showing it."

"Mr. Timkins is too zealous in his performance of what he thinks is his duty. If he had inquired of Mr. Jefferson, he would have allowed you to ride in style with the passengers."

Slocum doubted that but said nothing. Burlison wanted something or he would have been chucked into the San Diego courthouse iron cage by now.

"I find myself in a curious position." He licked his lips. "Would you care for some wine, Mr. Slocum? It is a French vintage. I selected it personally on a recent tour of the Provence region. That is the oldest in France and has a deserved reputation for producing the finest wines."

Slocum nodded. It didn't surprise him when the conductor fetched a cut crystal decanter and two glasses. He poured the bloodred wine with practiced ease, then stepped back.

His expression left nothing to the imagination. He wished for a glass, too.

"Yes, a fine vintage. To you, Mr. Slocum, and your heroism." Burlison lifted his glass, but Slocum left his on the table.

"I'd like to join you in that toast," Slocum said, "but the real hero deserves a taste of the wine more 'n I do." He looked at the conductor. For the briefest instant, astonishment flashed across his impassive face. Then a tiny smile curled the corners before he once more stood like a statue.

"Why, uh, yes, I suppose that is so. Pour yourself a glass, too, Jefferson."

Slocum perked up. The head of a railroad had agreed to share his wine with a black man. Whatever he wanted had to be big. If he played his cards right, Slocum thought he could leave San Diego not only without having a noose dropped around his neck but also with a few coins jingling in his pockets.

"To you, Mr. Slocum. And to you, Jefferson." Burlison's lips barely touched the rim of his glass.

Slocum and Jefferson knocked theirs back and let the wine trickle down their throats.

"Good," Slocum said.

"Yes, well, yes, it is good wine. Expensive."

Slocum waited.

"I am in a terrible hurry and must tend to business matters in San Francisco. Very important railroad business."

"Seems you are going the wrong direction if you're supposed to be in charge of the railroad in Texas."

"You are an astute man, Mr. Slocum." Burlison's words said one thing, but the exasperated look told another. "You have shown yourself to be capable in a gunfight and a trustworthy soul. You had no reason other than doing the right thing to come to the aid of Mr. Jefferson and the passengers, nor did you have to chase off the robbers trying to steal . . . well, let's say they were trying to steal something of great value to the railroad."

"Your wine's reward enough," Slocum said. "And a ticket to Texas." He looked up at the conductor.

"San Antonio," Jefferson said. "The company headquartah's in San Antonio."

"A ticket to San Antonio," Slocum said. Burlison's reaction confused him. Ordering such a rich and powerful man to give him a specific reward should have angered him. If anything, he looked relieved.

"You shall receive that and more, Mr. Slocum. I have lost five of my best men in the past week. All I require of you is to escort something of great value to San Antonio, something that was on the train you saved. I can only say that the robbers were ignorant of the true value carried in the car immediately behind the tender rather than the paltry few thousand in scrip in the mail car's safe."

Slocum grinned. He'd finally found out what was in the safe. Then his smile faded.

"I want you to escort my daughter, Marlene, safely to San Antonio, where her mother awaits."

3

"That's not the sort of job I take," Slocum said. He glanced at Jefferson. The conductor had put on his impassive face again, revealing nothing. Slocum had the feeling the man had something to do with the offer.

"You have the look of a man capable of taking care of himself—and others." Burlison finally drank the wine, taking it in a gulp as Slocum and Jefferson already had. He showed no more pleasure in its flavor or bouquet than they had. "I mentioned that my most able bodyguards were all lost."

"Kilt, kilt dead, Mistah Burlison. Come on out and say it. Mistah Slocum deserves to know."

"You're right," the railroad magnate said. "I have to go to San Francisco because of a messy business situation. The railroad is engaged in delicate negotiations to expand. If I can bring the warring parties together, we'll be unmatched in miles, freight, and passengers." He cleared his throat, motioned for Jefferson to pour more wine, and downed it before continuing. "My personal fortune depends on my success. Every penny I own is on the line, along with a great deal more. There is a faction opposed to this expansion that has tendered a ridiculous offer to buy the S&P. My absence would guarantee them ascendancy. If they succeed, I am ruined financially and the 'road is crippled."

"Who killed the bodyguards?" Slocum had no interest in the financial wheeling and dealing done by railroad men.

"The parties interested in preventing the merger will stop at nothing to get their way. When my guards refused to be bought, they were killed. Gunned down like mad dogs." Burlison shivered. Jefferson poured another glass of wine. "Attempts to kill me won't stop the deal that I am so ardently pursuing."

"But kidnapping your daughter would?"

"Yes, Mr. Slocum, it would. There is nothing I value more than my little girl. Even her mother is at a different level. Marlene is the apple of my eye. That's why I want her out of California and taken to Texas, where she can be better protected."

"Nobody's gunning for you there?"

"My enemies are Californian. While they have the resources to hire kidnappers anywhere, my estate in Texas is like a fortress, with an army of guards. Marlene is only in danger while she is traveling. Now," he said, finishing his wine in a final gulp, "you will be paid one hundred dollars and given a free ride to San Antonio in exchange for escorting my little girl there safely."

Slocum considered the man's situation. Morgan Burlison had to be desperate to tap someone he didn't know to perform such a task.

"Jefferson is a quick judge of men and says you are daring and trustworthy."

"With respect to your conductor, how's he know your clerk—"

"Mr. Timkins."

"How does he know that Timkins isn't right about me, that I was in the gang and had a falling-out?"

"I got to my present position judging men quickly. Timkins

is an idiot. Oh, he has his uses. He is single-minded when it comes to performing his duty, but he lacks imagination. He does not think through a situation. You are a man who lives inside his skull, Mr. Slocum, always thinking and looking for the proper solution to your problems. When a solution comes to you, you act. That's the person I need. A man who can put his plans into action because he knows he is right."

"I've known a passel of men who thought they were always right. They seldom were."

Burlison laughed without humor. "There was one in San Diego like that. Locked up in the iron cage but got out. Roy Bean was his name. Nobody ever convinced him when he was wrong. He became a judge in Texas. Pigheaded fool, but he got things done."

"Depends on what you want done, I reckon," Slocum said. He looked out the Pullman car window. The first pinks of dawn crept into the clouds. With daylight came the posses after him. And the bounty hunter. Big Joe impressed him as the kind of man who never stopped until he earned his bounty.

"Marlene is a good girl," Burlison said earnestly. "You protect her and deliver her into her ma's arms in San Antonio. I'll make it two hundred dollars."

"That's twice what I'm worth," Slocum said. He meant the posted reward that the bounty hunter sought. Burlison interpreted it differently.

"You'll be worth every penny. I'm ordering the Yuma Bullet to take you all the way to San Antonio."

"What happened to the train so that the robbers stopped it? If your daughter was in her car, I'd've thought the engineer would have plowed ahead through a barricade."

"They done removed a rail," Jefferson explained. "If'n Mad Tom'd kept on, the Yuma Bullet woulda been derailed."

"You have a crew replacing the rail?"

"By now it ought to be done. The Yuma Bullet will pull out, only two Pullman cars this time, a freight car, and the mail car along with the caboose. Mad Tom will highball it the entire way, stopping only for coal and water."

Leaving San Diego at top speed suited Slocum, but playing nanny to a little girl stuck in his craw. He said so.

"She'll be in good hands. Her maid will see to Marlene's personal needs. They have one car, you will have another, and in the freight car will be supplies."

"What of the mail car that the robbers wanted?"

"Ah, yes, you fear they will attempt to rob the train once more. With the supplies in the freight car, I will see that adequate firepower is provided. I would put that car with the other passenger cars on a later train, but the money has to be delivered to the Deming depot as quickly as possible."

"I'm one man against a gang, if they try to rob the train again. Even if they aren't out to kidnap your daughter, that much money's a lure as sure as honey draws flies."

"You keep trying to talk yourself out of it, Mr. Slocum. However, I have learned to read a man and his intentions. You argue to gain better terms, but you will accept my employment. Three hundred dollars."

Slocum heard someone say, "Done. Let's shake on it," before he realized he was the one speaking. His mouth had written an IOU he might have to pay with his life.

"Well met, sir. I know Marlene will be safe in your care." Burlison leaned over and pumped his hand. "Jefferson will be along. He can order any special supplies you require. Now, I must get on the rails to San Francisco if I am to be there by noon tomorrow."

Jefferson held the door for him. Slocum ducked through and hopped off the metal platform to the ground. The conductor trailed him, then wrapped an arm around his shoulders and lifted him easily off his feet, spun him about, and put him down as light as a feather.

The clang of a car coupling with another was followed quickly by Burlison's Pullman rolling along where Slocum had stood an instant before.

"Thanks. You kept me from getting run over." He watched Burlison leave, the man already bent over his desk and scribbling as the car rolled through the yards.

"You gotta learn what all dem sounds mean. Now you know what you want for da trip?"

"I'll leave that up to you. Get me a case of rifles and ammo. I'll need my six-shooter back and ammo for it."

"Colt Navy .36 caliber," Jefferson said. "I know my guns."

"I suspect you stand by them, too," Slocum said. He pressed his hand onto his bare hip. He felt undressed without his six-shooter. "I need it back right now."

"You was hitchin' a ride on da Yuma Bullet 'cuz you is runnin', ain't you?"

"I am," Slocum said. He saw no reason to lie to the conductor.

His honesty made Jefferson nod slowly, then grin.

"Me and you, we is gonna git along jist fine. You tell dat ticket clerk McIlheny to give you yo' gun. He got it. Ammo, too."

"Where can I find Marlene Burlison?"

Jefferson shook his head and said, "I kin find guns and most ever'thing else. No way I know where she is. We been back in depot long 'nuff foah her to git into a shitload of trouble."

"What about her nanny?"

"Nanny? Nanny!" Jefferson walked off, shaking his head and laughing at some joke Slocum failed to understand.

Slocum looked around the rail yard and felt exposed. The two railroad bulls wouldn't bother him but he *felt* danger coming. He went to the depot, climbed the creaking steps, and pressed his face against the bars to the ticket agent's booth. A man had his feet hiked to a desk and chin to chest, snored loudly.

"Are you McIlheny?" His loud question caused the man to jerk around, his feet sliding off the desk and almost throwing him onto the floor.

"No tickets for another hour."

"Burlison said you had my six-shooter and some ammo to go with it."

McIlheny got to his feet and came to the window, rubbing his eyes. He thrust his face so it was only inches from Slocum's.

"Timkins gave me a gun he took off a train robber."

"Timkins is an idiot. I stopped the robbery."

"Yeah, well, you can say that again. Mr. Burlison wanted you to have this back?" From under the window ledge the clerk grabbed Slocum's holster with the ebony-handled Colt thrust in it. He added a box of cartridges for the rechambered pistol.

"Where can I find his daughter?" Slocum strapped on the six-gun, then took time to reload. The remaining shells he dropped into his coat pocket. He had the feeling he would be needing them.

"Miss Burlison?" The clerk snickered, then sobered. "Can't rightly say. She's supposed to be in her car waiting to pull out again for Texas, but I heard tell she got bored after settin' there for all of ten minutes. That means she went into town."

"How old is she?" Slocum slid his pistol back into the holster. "I got the impression she wasn't too old. She has a nanny."

"Miss Mulligan's not her nanny. She's her maid."

Slocum wondered if his job got easier or harder. He had thought the girl was young from the way her pa talked about her. An older girl—a young woman—presented a different challenge if she went into San Diego to kick up her heels.

He left McIlheny laughing at him. Slocum noticed that happened a lot around the railroad people. Marlene Burlison's fancy Pullman car had been put onto a siding near the Yuma Bullet locomotive and a crew worked to repair some small problem beneath it. He asked one of the workers where Marlene Burlison could be found.

The man scratched his head with an oily finger, then said,

"I seen her and her traveling companion leave in a carriage, just 'fore sunrise. They was heading toward town." The man turned secretive and leaned closer to whisper, "I betcha they was going out to find Miss Burlison's beau. Rumor has it he's a wild one, wilder than a Texas tornado."

"Where does he hang out?"

"Never seen him and haven't heard anything but rumors, but a fine lady like that would be noticed no matter where she went."

Slocum considered finding a train going in some other direction, jumping it, and getting the hell away from what had quickly turned into an irksome job. He hadn't laid eyes on the girl and already he had to track her down and drag her from her boyfriend's bed. From the look of the Yuma Bullet, it was about ready to build up a head of steam and pull out again.

He started into town on foot, then slowed when he saw a carriage and driver nearby. The driver held up a newspaper to catch the morning light but put it down when Slocum approached.

"You want a ride into town? Only two bits."

"You take two ladies in not long ago?" Slocum saw the way the driver tensed.

"What if I did?"

"Mr. Burlison is vice president of the S&P and will be grateful—very grateful—if you take me where you took them."

"He's got the reputation for being a generous man," the driver said.

"As generous as he is, I'm that impatient to find the ladies. It wouldn't do if they missed their train." Slocum moved his coattail away from his six-shooter.

"I can bill Mr. Burlison?"

"You take me to the ladies and you can charge for the return trip, too. Double your rate."

"Double," the driver mused as he folded his newspaper.

He lifted his butt off the driver's seat, slid the paper under him, and dropped back. "You climb on in and let's roll."

Slocum hopped into the carriage and was pressed back into the seat as they rattled away at a trot.

"Mind if I look at the newspaper?"

"Go on. I got it straight off the press so the ink's smeary. But you can still read most of it." The driver lifted, snagged the paper, and tossed it back to Slocum.

He tensed when he read the front page. The reward up in San Dismas for his capture had been upped to five hundred dollars. Big Joe Joseph wouldn't be the only bounty hunter itching to collect that reward. The sketch with the story had smeared so the driver would never identify Slocum from it, even if he paid that much attention to his passenger with the lure of billing the railroad for private carriage service dangling in front of him.

One smaller article caught Slocum's attention. The man who had killed Harry Goodwin had been cornered and filled full of lead. Whether that was good news for Slocum wore on him. The deputies otherwise occupied with finding the killer of a prominent citizen's son now could hunt for the San Dismas bank robber and murderer. Five hundred dollars was more than a deputy made in a full year. Even if ten of them split the reward, that was one hell of a bender in the making.

"Here's the place. It's all quiet now."

"Wait here. I won't be long." Slocum hopped down and went to the front door of the house. He hesitated to knock, wondering if the driver had led him astray bringing him to a cathouse.

Realizing he had nowhere else to search at the moment, Slocum rapped sharply. The door opened inward to reveal an elegantly dressed woman with rouged cheeks and blond hair piled high. Tiny specks that Slocum took to be rhinestones hidden in the hair glittered in the morning sun. Sharp blue eyes fixed on him. A broad smile crossed her lips and revealed dimples.

"Why, do come in, sir," she said. "I'd thought the day couldn't get any better. I was wrong." She stepped back to let him enter.

Beyond Slocum saw a small sitting room. A small bar with a half-dozen bottles of whiskey and brandy stretched under a stained glass window now brilliant with a new day's light. The furnishings were as expensive as the madam bidding him to enter.

"I'm looking for a lady. Two ladies," he quickly amended.

"I'm sure you can handle two. At the same time or separately? Oh, it doesn't matter. I hope you'll consider me to be one of them, and I just know any number of my other ladies will suit your . . . tastes."

"Marlene Burlison," he said. "Is she here?"

"Names aren't important." The madam gave him a more critical examination now. He wasn't dressed for such an expensive whorehouse and showed none of the manners most appearing at the door would.

"They are to Morgan Burlison. Her father. You must have heard of him."

"I don't want any trouble."

"I'm sure you and your ladies dish out only pleasure. You have your profession and I have my job. Marlene Burlison. Where is she?"

"Fenton!" The woman spun, her skirts making soft, whispering, come-hither sounds. "Fenton, where are they?"

A man half Slocum's size came from a back room. From the way he dressed—and clanked—he was a gambler and armed to the teeth. Slocum saw two ivory knife handles poking out from inner pockets, and bulges gave away the hiding places of a pair of small-caliber pistols.

"In the back, but I don't think it's a good idea to disturb them. They only just settled in."

Slocum pushed past the madam and came even with Fenton. When the gambler's eyes flickered down to his side, he betrayed himself. Slocum swung, his punch hitting the man on the cheek. The gambler dropped to a couch, holding his bruised face.

"Touch a knife or gun and it'll be the last thing you do."

Fenton started to straighten his left arm. From the way his sleeve creased, he wore a spring-loaded contraption that shoved a pistol into his hand. Slocum had his Colt out and coming down hard on the man's wrist as the derringer popped out. The pistol fell to the heavily carpeted floor without so much as a whisper.

"Fenton, let him be."

"Yeah, Fenton, let me be." Slocum turned the six-shooter slightly so the man peered down the bore. The Colt was a smaller caliber than most men packed now, but it had to look like the mouth of a water barrel.

Seeing the gambler subside, Slocum went down a long hall, then turned. Rooms on either side told him the place was bigger than he thought. It might cover half the block. Quick looks into the rooms as he went showed little activity. Most held only the sleeping ladies of the night, their work done until sunset. But one door caught his eye. Silver filigree had been set into the wood, marking it as different from the cribs. He eased open the door.

Inside a woman sat in a chair with hands folded in her lap, looking uneasy, while another pressed her eye against a wall. The woman in the chair cried out. The other didn't budge but only hissed for her to be quiet. Slocum stepped in and saw the one girl peered through a spyhole.

"What's in the other room?" he asked.

"He's about to—" The woman realized her blond companion had not asked the question. She pulled away and stared at Slocum. "Who are you?"

"Are you Marlene Burlison? Your pa hired me to escort you to San Antonio."

"I . . . no, she's Marlene. I'm Sarah Jane Mulligan."

"Miss Mulligan," Slocum said, touching the brim of his hat. The dark-haired woman looked flushed and out of breath. Her ample breasts heaved up and down under a bodice that appeared chaste at first glance but which delicate lacework revealed a considerable amount of snowy white breasts. Her waist was small enough for Slocum to reach around with both hands and have his fingers touch. Her blue eyes shone brightly and contrasted with her midnight mane, making her seem wild and unchecked.

He went to the peephole. However the madam had done it, the view into the next room was panoramic. A man positioned behind a naked woman bent over the bed was about to enter her from the rear.

"Learning anything?" he asked as he backed away a step and pulled down a small wooden disk nailed to the wall, blocking the spyhole.

"Not really," she said. She brushed back her dark hair and sucked in a deep breath to further enhance her bosoms. She put one hand on a cocked hip and gave him a come-hither look that would have produced a hard-on if he hadn't been so focused on doing the job Morgan Burlison had given him.

"Miss Burlison," he said to the woman in the chair, "the train leaves very soon." Pulling his eyes from her maid was hard, especially with the way Sarah Jane licked her lips so wantonly. In spite of what she said, she had learned a great deal watching the sexual goings-on in the other room.

"It won't leave without us, me," the blonde said. She looked up boldly at Slocum, then dropped eyes as green as his own to her folded hands. The monetary burst of defiance faded fast. She was a complete opposite to her maid.

She wasn't anything like Slocum had expected. When he figured out Marlene Burlison was a young woman and not a child needing a nanny, he expected her to look like her pa.

The blond woman had a finely boned face and healthy complexion showing she spent some time away from indoor pursuits such as watching coupling. Her hair was mussed but was clean and shone like gold in the dim light from the oil lamp on a nearby table. Those fearful eyes darted back at him and then more fearlessly met his gaze. She wasn't going to back down now. Watching her change from mouse to lion warned Slocum he had his hands full with her mercurial moods.

"Let's go." Slocum took her by the elbow and got the blonde to her feet. She was taller than he'd expected, perhaps five foot five, and trim, but with a full figure that would have made her a favorite in the cathouse.

Her dress was expensive but without ornamentation, as fitting for a woman out for a night of being a Peeping Tom. She had a dark cloak draped over the back of her chair. Slocum took it and, with a flourish, spun it around so it settled about her shoulders. She never took her eyes off him. A smile slowly grew that lit her face.

"Thank you," she said. She turned but Slocum kept his arm about her. She tensed and pushed back to look at her maid. "We must go, you know."

"I want to stay. It was just getting interesting."

"Sarah Jane," she said sternly. "We must go. Now."

"How do we know he's who he says? That your father sent him for us?"

"Stay and watch or come along," Slocum said. "Nothing was said about seeing Miss Burlison's maid on the train." He herded the woman ahead of him. Behind them, the maid sputtered.

"You can't leave me. I . . . I have my job, too. To look after Marlene!"

"Some job you were doing," he said. "Why'd you allow her to come here?"

He kept the two women moving down the hall to the

sitting room, where the madam dabbed gently at Fenton's bruised cheek.

"You struck him?" Marlene asked.

"Yes, Miss Burlison, I did."

"He's harmless," Sarah Jane said.

Slocum wasn't in the mood to argue. Any man who carried as many different types of weapons as Fenton was anything but harmless. He was a man accustomed to using the knives and pistols when his luck ran out—or he was caught cheating.

"Do come back," the madam said as the women left. "Without your bodyguard next time."

"It has been wonderful, Lady Jessica." Sarah Jane bowed slightly to the madam, stopped, and then said, "You should pay her, Marlene. It's only fair."

"What, oh, yes, of course." The blonde fumbled and found a pocket in the cloak Slocum hadn't noticed when he had helped her on with it. She passed over a sizable wad of greenbacks, then added a few more, saying, "For Fenton's trouble."

Slocum kept Marlene moving until they got outside. The waiting driver jumped down and extended his hand to help her into the carriage.

"Mr. Burlison is certainly hiring better-looking employees," Sarah Jane said, coming up behind Slocum. She gripped down hard on his buttocks.

Slocum hardly noticed.

"Get in. The driver will take you back to the train. I have some business to attend to."

"Will you be long?" Sarah Jane giggled. "Of course you are."

Slocum shot the driver a hard look. The man swallowed nervously, then snapped the reins to get the horse pulling back to the depot.

He waited for them to turn a corner and disappear before

he drew his six-shooter and started across the street to where Big Joe had a man pinned against the wall, interrogating him. Halfway across, the bounty hunter sensed something wrong, shoved aside the man, and whirled around to face Slocum. He went for the scattergun he had slung from a leather strap over his shoulder.

4

Slocum took two quick steps forward and swung his six-shooter in a wide arc that ended on the side of the bounty hunter's head. The dull crunch told of bones breaking, but Big Joe didn't go down. The blow staggered him, but he kept fumbling for the shotgun. Slocum took another step forward and whirled the pistol around backhanded and landed the barrel on the other side of Big Joe's head.

This knocked him to the ground, his eyes rolling up in his head. Although more unconscious than aware, he clung to the shotgun. His finger spastically jerked and both barrels discharged. Slocum danced away, as if he could outrun the buckshot loaded into that deadly weapon. He winced as one ball ripped away part of his boot top and took flesh just above it away in a bloody spray.

For all his minor injury hurt, he saw the bounty hunter was in a worse way. Big Joe had fired his shotgun into his own meaty thigh. Blood oozed through the filthy buckskin pants and turned into a gory mud.

"You might have killed yourself," Slocum said, kneeling down. "If you blasted an artery, you're a goner."

The man's eyes flickered open. He lurched upward, trying to bite Slocum.

"You got the wrong man," Slocum said. "Take that to your grave. You shouldn't have come for me because I had nothing to do with the killings or the robbery."

He rocked back and stood. Aware of a crowd gathering, he slid his Colt Navy back into his holster.

"What happened?" asked a man who had turned white at the sight of so much blood and shredded flesh.

"His shotgun went off accidentally," Slocum said. He let the crowd press closer to Big Joe and push him away.

He hobbled a mite as he made his way from the circle of people, loudly speculating as to the bounty hunter's fate. When he turned the corner where the carriage with Marlene and her maid had disappeared, he tried to walk faster. The sound of a train whistle echoed through the streets. It might have been the Yuma Bullet readying for its express trip to San Antonio or it could have been another train, a freight train, or another passenger train.

If he missed the Yuma Bullet, he was out the three hundred dollars Morgan Burlison had promised him for babysitting his daughter on a milk run. His boot squishing from the puddling blood, he reached the depot. The train had connected the Pullman, freight, and mail cars but no smoke puffed out of the locomotive's stack. Two men in filthy overalls stood beside the engine's front wheel, pointing and shouting at each other. The engineer sat on the step leading up to the cab. Behind him the fireman gripped a railing and swung out to watch the fight.

Slocum hobbled over.

"What's the problem?" he asked Mad Tom. The origin of the man's moniker was apparent. The engineer turned so his face pointed off at an angle but one eye fixed on Slocum. Not only was he walleyed but the other eye had a milky film over it. Just looking at him gave Slocum the collywobbles.

"Now that there's a bone of contention," Mad Tom said.

His raspy voice added to his creepy aspect. He spat a black gobbet that hit the ground, sizzled, and vanished amid the cinders. "One of them thinks we burnt a bearing. The other's certain sure the whole danged drive wheel's got to be replaced. Me, I'm leanin' toward it bein' neither of them."

"Yeah, me and Tom think there's an oil reservoir leak."

"Replace an itty-bitty cylinder and we'd be good as gold." Mad Tom spat again.

"How long before we get rolling?"

"Well now, seein' as how you're the gent Mr. Burlison hired on to look after his lovely daughter, you got a right to know that." Mad Tom wiped his lips on an oily rag. "The answer's real easy. I don't know."

"Miss Burlison back in her car?"

"'Spect she is. Her and her cute li'l handmaid drove up all prissy and spittin' fire not twenty minutes back."

Pain lancing all the way up into his groin now, Slocum limped to the second Pullman but didn't mount the metal steps. He swung about and sat heavily. Wincing, he tried to work off his boot but the pain in his leg made him stop. He looked up over his shoulder when he heard a small gasp.

"Whatever happened to you?" Marlene Burlison stared at the bloody pant leg, her green eyes as big as saucers.

"Cut myself up a mite," Slocum said. He had no reason to explain what had happened since that required him to tell how a bounty hunter had come sniffing along his back trail.

"I'll get some water and bandages." She vanished into the Pullman car.

Slocum went back to working off the boot. He poured a goodly amount of blood out onto the cinders, where it was sucked up instantly. Pulling back the cloth plastered to his leg exposed the shallow wound. As he'd thought, the shot had caused more blood than damage.

"Move over," Marlene said, stepping past him as she exited the car. Her skirts swirled and momentarily suffocated him.

Then she was kneeling in front of him, dabbing at the dried blood and gently examining the crease. He stared at her. For a rich man's daughter, she showed no revulsion at the wound or tending it.

"There's no need for you to take care of it," Slocum said.

"It's not serious at all. I've seen worse. I did worse to myself when I fell out of a tree when I was eight. I caught my chin on a limb and it tore a six-inch gash. I thought I was going to die. It wasn't in the least painful, but I bled like a stuck pig."

Slocum reached over, put his finger under her chin, and lifted. A faint white scar running from her shoulder across her neck and up under her chin showed she wasn't fibbing.

"No pain at all? A cut that bad on a little girl's neck should have hurt like the devil."

"My pa always treated me as if I were his son. 'No tears, girl,' he always said. Ma stitched it up." She looked a bit sheepish, then turned her face up to Slocum. "He held my hand while Ma did the sewing and he was right. It hurt but I didn't cry."

"That was brave of you," Slocum said. "I reckon your pa worked his way up in the railroad?"

He thought he had poked her with a pin. She recoiled, then settled back down to complete the cleansing before expertly bandaging his leg.

"Pa has always been a hard worker. There. Your boot's a mess but your leg's going to be fine."

"I've been hurt worse than this," Slocum said.

"I suspect you have." Marlene looked away as if she were embarrassed at what she was thinking.

Slocum had to wonder what that might be to bring roses to her cheeks and a quickening to her breathing. He found her enticing, but he knew better than to fool around with the boss's daughter. Even if she wanted to fool around with a drifter and a man with a bloody wound in his leg.

"I'll go clean up."

"There's a bathtub in this car. You—" Marlene bit off

her words when Sarah Jane came running up, waving her arms to get the girl's attention. "Whatever does she want now?" Marlene spoke so low that she meant the words only for herself, but Slocum overheard.

"We're going to find out, I reckon."

Marlene jumped and stared at him in panic. Then she settled down and only nodded.

"I've just got a 'gram from . . . from your father, Marlene. He's returning and wants us to wait until he arrives."

"That's not much of a problem," Slocum said. "The Yuma Bullet's got mechanical problems. It'll take a spell to figure out what's wrong, then fix it."

"My, aren't we the knowing one, Mr. Slocum? Or can I call you John?"

"John's my name," he said. Sarah Jane's blue eyes danced with merriment, as if she had duped him into admitting something wicked. For all that, Slocum would pit her thoughts with those of Marlene. Both women had more than getting to San Antonio on their minds.

The peepshow at the whorehouse showed that. Sarah Jane had been actively enjoying the sight of the amorous activity in the next room. He looked again at Marlene. She squared her shoulders and stood. She handed the basin with the bloody water to Sarah Jane.

"Take care of this, will you? Mr. Slocum injured himself and I tended his wound."

"Did you now? Aren't you all the nurse?" Sarah Jane bent over and peered at the neatly tied bandage. "You used my petticoat!"

"It was convenient," Marlene said.

"Get on with your business, John," Sarah Jane said. "Marlene and I have to prepare for Mr. Burlison. He'll be back in about an hour."

"Why's that? He was in an all-fired hurry to get to San Francisco on business. It was like somebody had lit a torch under him."

"You wanted to say 'set his ass on fire,' didn't you, John?" Sarah Jane spoke with obvious malice, wanting him to apologize.

"I say what I mean." He saw the flicker of a smile on Marlene's lips that disappeared as quickly as it was born. "You ladies had better get ready. I'll do the same."

He held out his hand to help Marlene up the steps into their Pullman car. For some reason, Slocum didn't extend the same courtesy to Sarah Jane even though she pressed close. She made a point of tossing out the water, brushing against him, then looking at Marlene to see if the girl objected. Marlene waited quietly at the door into the car. Her impassive face showed no trace of whatever emotion her maid tried to spark.

As Sarah Jane scampered up the steps, Marlene went inside. The door slammed, leaving Slocum to wonder why Marlene had ever hired the girl. What drove Sarah Jane was obvious. If Slocum snapped his fingers, he could have her under the blanket in an instant. As sexy as she was, he knew he would have a good time and give her one, as well. But her behavior would only lead to trouble. Morgan Burlison wasn't the sort to put up with debauchery in his employees. The idea that Sarah Jane gave a bad example for his daughter would send Burlison into a rage Slocum wanted to avoid.

He hobbled away to find a water barrel near the depot. It took the better part of a half hour to scrub off the blood from his boot. When he pulled it on, it felt tight and required him to walk around to soften the wet leather and mold the boot to his foot once more. If he got shot in another month or so, the blood would drain out a hole in the sole. Right now the hole came close to poking all the way through, but enough leather remained to keep him from blistering. After Burlison paid him for escorting his daughter to San Antonio, there'd be plenty of money for a new pair of boots. Slocum had heard of a cobbler there who'd make a custom pair for what this pair had cost off the shelf of a general store up in Sacramento.

Testing his leg, he climbed the steps to the depot and pressed his face against the bars at the ticket agent's booth once more. This time McIlheny hunched over the telegraph key, sending the dots and dashes along the wire to satisfy what must have been a dozen customers.

"You got word on Burlison's arrival?" Slocum called.

McIlheny kept at his work as he said, "An hour. Maybe less. His train broke down ten miles out of town and is limping back to the yard for repair."

"He fit to be tied over the delay?"

"I got the 'gram. Damn near melted the wires it was so hot." McIlheny looked up. "You better mind your p's and q's. When he gets all het up, he and his daughter argue 'bout nothing." The clerk sniffed. "Hell, they argue about everything. Anybody caught in the cross fire gets their head blown off."

"Thanks for the warning." Slocum took out his pocket watch and compared it to the station's Regulator clock ticking balefully. The times matched close enough.

He walked to the edge of the depot platform and looked down the few feet to the ground. Testing his leg now gave him more confidence later. He jumped. The impact sent a shock up into his hip but otherwise supported him fine. Slocum walked fast to the crew working on the Yuma Bullet. Two men were beneath the wheels, one banging away with a small sledgehammer, while another man stood nearby, holding an oilcan and looking bored.

The fireman had gone, but Mad Tom sat on a step cleaning his filthy fingernails with a knife. He never looked up as Slocum stopped in front of him.

"No idea," Tom said.

Slocum had to laugh. The question was an obvious one, and Mad Tom didn't have to read minds to know.

"Anything I can do?"

"You know anything 'bout engines?" Mad Tom glanced at Slocum before returning to his futile work.

"I see how things fit together pretty well. I worked a spell along the Mississippi as a dock hand and saw something of how steam capstans worked."

"Be better if they'd let you fool 'round with the steam engines below deck. I got my start there, then saw how the riverboats was a dyin' breed so I went to KC and lied my way onto an engine as fireman so I could work up to my exalted position of train driver." He finished his cleaning, wiped the point on his overalls, then yelled, "Hersch, you got help comin'. First-rate mechanic what'll show you how stupid you've been." Mad Tom pointed with the knife blade for Slocum to get to work.

The man with the oilcan used the spigot to indicate a spot just behind the front wheels.

"You know shit 'bout a Prairie?"

"It's a 2-6-2," Slocum said. "Two lead wheels don't do anything but keep the front on the tracks. The next six do the work. Two rear wheels under the cab support a goodly portion of the weight from the firebox."

"You know more 'n I do, then," the oiler said. "I know the damn thing can't run if it falls off the tracks. Seen one try once. It blowed itself up when it hit the ground." He bent and yelled under the engine, "Hersch, we got ourselves an expert."

Slocum wondered at how easy it was to become an expert just because he had ridden enough trains in his day and gotten drunk with enough engineers to hear about wheels. He pulled off his holster and hung it from a knob protruding from the boiler. Wiggling on his back, he felt the cut of cinders against his shirt. He tore shreds out of it, but the money he'd get from Burlison would pay for a new shirt as well as decent boots. The scent of hot oil and burned steel made his nostrils flare. A quick swipe across his eyes cleared them of tears forming against the fumes.

"What's the problem?" He saw that Hersch had wiped clean everything on the locomotive's underbelly to home in on the trouble. In spite of what Mad Tom and the oiler had proclaimed, Slocum knew little about the workings of the engine. Nothing looked out of place to him.

"Don't know. Been workin' on these steel monsters nigh on ten years. Never the same thing breakin' twice. When Tom hit the brakes to keep from goin' off the tracks, somethin' popped and spewed oil ever'where. Just can't tell what that somethin' is."

Hersch wiped some more at a greasy cylinder and watched for new oil. He scooted toward the rear of the engine and stopped near the middle of the drive wheels to repeat his wipe-wait spot check.

"Boss, I gotta go. You have plenny of help with him."

Slocum heard rather than saw the other man who worked even farther toward the rear of the locomotive.

"Get on outta here, Lew. But you're standin' me a round tonight. Two!"

"Next payday, Hersch, next payday. I'm tapped out right now." Lew scrapped his way from underneath the engine, leaving Slocum alongside his boss.

"What he said about tapped out," Slocum said. "You tried tapping on the cylinders to see if one sounds different?"

"Naw, just huntin' fer leaks. This here's an oil reservoir fer the front drive wheel." Hersch banged on it with a wrench. "This other one's for the mid wheel." He rapped it a couple times, hesitated, and repeated. "I'll be switched. That sounds empty." A third time for Slocum's benefit confirmed the reservoir being dry.

"Have your oiler fill it up and let's watch." Slocum took a spare rag that had been stuffed into Hersch's overall pocket and rubbed the small tank clean. "Looks rusty." He pointed to a connection.

"They're all like that, even the ones what run in the desert. Water from condensed steam and spilled water tank fillings gets up under and ain't nowhere to go so it rusts fast."

Hersch ordered the man with the oilcan to empty it and then refill to keep pouring.

"Danged thing's got a thirst," he said. "But lookee there. A leak just like an Irishman spittin' chaw from 'twixt his front teeth."

"Can you replace it?"

"Have to. Looks to be a split in the side of the cylinder, so teeny it only shows itself when oil's leakin' out. It comes out, catches on pistons, and that's why it was spattered to hell and gone underneath. You're one smart fella."

"Slocum," he introduced himself.

"I'll have Lew buy you a round, too." He yelled out for the oiler to fetch another oil reservoir. It took a full minute before the man understood.

"Do you have a spare in your warehouse?" Slocum asked.

"Got a dozen of 'em. When they fail, they usually do it like a Fourth of July firecracker. Sparks and fire and enough hissing to make even a grizzled ole engineer think he's headin' fer the Pearly Gates."

"How long'll it take to get this out and the new one installed?"

"Dipshit out there's back with the spare. If you help as good as you diagnose, we'll be out from under here in a half hour, and I'll be pleased as punch to call you Doc Slocum."

The new reservoir appeared between the front and the middle drive wheels. Slocum wrestled it around, aligned it to lift up into place when Hersch freed the busted one. The mechanic grunted as he applied more power to the wrench. A shower of oil brought forth a curse. The reservoir dropped down, bending its piping. A screech of agonized metal was followed by a human scream of pain.

The reservoir had broken off and crushed Hersch's chest. All Slocum could see was the man's blood mixing with the oil.

5

Hersch stopped yelling after the cylinder plunged down into his chest. Slocum saw white ribs poking out amid the flood of oil and gore. The man twitched feebly and tried to push away.

"Hang on," Slocum said, scooting closer until his shoulder pressed into Hersch.

Bracing his shoulder against the railroad ties beneath him, he began pushing. He tried not to jerk hard. If he yanked the oily cylinder out of the man's chest too fast, he'd die. But Slocum found his muscles screaming with exertion. He barely budged the cylinder.

"What's goin' on?" Mad Tom sounded more pissed than wanting real information.

"Hersch is pinned. Piece of metal shot him clean through like an Indian arrow. Can't get it pushed away from him."

The engineer scooted under the engine, wiggling like a fish tossed out of the river onto a rocky bank. He added his strength to Slocum's but still couldn't budge the cylinder more than an inch. Hersch moaned louder now, blood spraying from his mouth.

"You get ready to drag him out," Slocum said.

"What you gonna do, Slocum?"

Slocum released his grip on the impaling cylinder and rolled onto his belly. He moved back until his shoulders shoved into the metal. Using both arms and legs, he lifted himself straight up like a cat stretching its back. The metal squeaked a mite, then began to yield under his onslaught. Slocum closed his eyes, gritted his teeth, and shoved even harder until the world started turning black. The effort caused his head to spin and his vision to blur.

He pushed even harder. The metal cut into his shoulders and liquid flowed sluggishly down his arms. It might have been oil. More likely it was his own blood.

He vented a loud cry and expended all his strength in a single surge.

"Got him."

Slocum held the cylinder for as long as he could, then lowered it, aware that he might end up like Hersch. The oil reservoir dug into the railroad tie beside him. Then he collapsed. Every ounce of energy had been spent. Facedown, he tried to move. Nothing happened when he kicked his legs or flailed his arms. Then he began sliding along, cinders cutting into his chest and cheek. Arching his back as much as he could, he kept more of the clinkers from slashing away at his face.

Strong hands rolled him over. He blinked. He stared straight up into the sun.

"You danged fool. Get outta the way." Mad Tom's ugly face blocked the direct sun.

"I swear, these boys're dumber than dirt. Lew shoulda knowed better 'n to point up at the sun like that. Can you set up, Slocum?"

He gripped Tom's hand and sat up. He winced at the pain lancing through his back.

"Not as bad as the time I flopped in a clump of prickly

pear cactus," Slocum said. To his surprise, he wasn't lying. Moving about restored his strength.

When Tom helped him to his feet, he was as steady as could be.

"How's Hersch?"

"Got him over in the shade and McIlheny goin' fer a doctor." Mad Tom looked at Slocum curiously. "Or are you a doc, too?"

"What do you mean?" Slocum brushed himself off. He certainly needed a new shirt. This one hung in bloody tatters on his back.

"Hersch keeps callin' fer Doc Slocum. That you?"

"A joke. Tell him you're sending for a vet since that's all he deserves."

Tom chuckled. "Don't know that a vet's not a better choice fer keepin' him alive. Never seen a vet with a bad bedside manner nor a real doctor with a good one."

Slocum started to check Hersch himself but two men lifted him onto a wood plank and carted him away to a waiting wagon.

"You saved his life," Tom said. "You mighta done yerself in, but you stuck with him."

"Thought it was my fault," Slocum said. "I found the problem and then it fell on top of him."

"So you kin fix the ole Yuma Bullet?"

"I'd like it better if somebody else tried. I can tell them what's wrong."

"Lew! Lew, dammit, git your ass over here. You listen real good to Doc Slocum an' do what he says, you hear?"

Slocum told Lew and the oiler what had to be done. Lew looked apprehensive, considering what had happened to Hersch, but the oiler readily scampered under the big engine. Lew trailed him but within minutes they were arguing over the best way to install the new reservoir Slocum had laid in place.

While they worked, Slocum walked slowly to the depot and sat on the second step. He held out his hands. They shook. He waited for the reaction to pass. By the time it did, an engine had pulled up fifty yards away. Slocum returned to the Yuma Bullet, took his gun belt from the knob where he'd hung it, and strapped it on. No trace of tremor remained as he slipped the pistol in and out of the leather a few times.

"There he is, Mr. Burlison."

Slocum whirled, ready to throw down. His nerves quieted when he saw Mad Tom hurrying alongside the railroad vice president.

"Is it true, Slocum? By damn, is it true?" Morgan Burlison stopped a foot away and stared hard at him.

"Depends on what's been said."

"It's true. Every word of it, sir," Mad Tom assured him. "I swear it on my mother's grave."

"I've never heard Tom go on like this before. Hell, I never even knew he had a mother." Burlison thrust out his hand. For a moment Slocum wondered what he was supposed to do. Then he shook. Oil dripped from his palm and onto the man's fancy lace cuff, but Burlison didn't flinch away or even notice the filth. "I knew you were the right man for the job."

"Your daughter's back—"

Burlison cut him off, still pumping his hand.

"Marlene can wait. I heard how you saved a man's life and then fixed the Yuma Bullet. Those are the qualities I admire. Selfless, courageous."

"He risked his own life, Mr. Burlison. Ain't seen anyone do that in a month of Sundays," said Tom. "He saved Hersch, and he got the engine repaired. We're 'bout ready to aim the Bullet for San Antonio."

"Good, Tom, very good." Burlison finally released Slocum's hand and clapped the engineer on the shoulder. "You go see to things, won't you? I want a moment with Slocum."

"Sure thing, sir. Goin' right now." Mad Tom hurried off,

shouting to anyone who would listen about Slocum's heroism.

"He's a good man, Tom Haney. You're a good man, too, Slocum. I had to come back to get my own engine repaired. If I didn't need you looking after Marlene, I'd have you on that chore." He slapped Slocum on the back as he had the engineer. Slocum saw it coming and didn't wince. Burlison's hand came away bloody and flecked with cinders. "I need to talk to my daughter a bit. Her telegram made me wonder what she's been up to. Can you tell me, Slocum?"

"She's been acting the proper lady, sir. Her maid's a bit of a hellion, though."

Burlison's eyebrows arched. "Sarah Jane? Are we talking about the same girl? Sarah Jane was hired to hold down my daughter's high spirits. My wife and I interviewed dozens of young ladies before deciding on her."

Slocum thought that the daughter's wild ways might have been passed along to Sarah Jane but said nothing.

"I escorted them back to the train."

"Escorted?"

"They'd gone into town to do some sightseeing. It wasn't anything that could get them into trouble," Slocum said, working to keep his face impassive. He had won big poker pots that way. This lie took all his skill.

"I respect your desire not to get my daughter into trouble, sir," Burlison said.

"You hired me to keep her out of trouble. That's what I'm doing."

Burlison slapped him again on the back and laughed. "Good man. You go clean up while I talk to my daughter."

"Depending on when the Yuma Bullet leaves, I need to get into town to buy some clothes." Before he could ask Burlison for an advance on the promised pay, the man waved him off.

"I'll have none of that. Jefferson can fetch you some of my discarded clothing. It should fit you reasonably well."

He stepped back and studied Slocum critically. "Can't do anything about the boots. My feet are considerably smaller than yours, but a shirt, coat, and vest and pants can serve you. Sarah Jane is adept with a needle. She can tailor the clothing for you on the way across the Sonora Desert. That's a boring, barren stretch of hot sand. Utterly boring. Nothing ever happens there that's worth mentioning."

He went off muttering to himself. Slocum took a deep breath and found himself a little woozy. From the tickling down his back, he realized he was still bleeding. With the earlier loss of blood from Big Joe's buckshot, he needed a thick juicy steak to build up his strength. At the moment peeling off the filthy duds and getting cleaned up would have to do.

He went to the second Pullman car and made his way up the iron steps. He heard a muffled argument between Burlison and Marlene in the other car. Going in, he stopped and stared, thinking he had entered Marlene's car by mistake. But she and her father were in the other, and this was hooked up in front of the mail car, indicating it was of lesser importance. If this was where he had to endure the Sonora Desert and the rest of the trip to Texas, he was in tall clover.

He stooped and tested the softness of the couch along one wall. It was a sight better than sleeping on the hard ground under the stars with nothing more than a threadbare blanket over his shoulders. Moving toward the rear of the car, he found a small bathroom, a copper-plated tub set to one side. A stove outside was perfect for heating not only water but the entire car if there had been a need. Crossing the desert in late spring reduced the need to use the stove. And that presented Slocum with a dilemma. He needed to haul water for the tub and heat it in a stove lacking fuel.

"There's plenny o' coal from the tender."

Slocum turned to see the conductor with clothing draped over his arm. Jefferson dropped it to a chair.

"Mistah Burlison he said that was foah you. Ain't never heard tell o' him givin' 'way his clothes before."

"I ruined what I was wearing." Slocum turned to show his back.

"Lordy, you did a deed. I'll get watah heatin' and you set yo'sef down in the tub. Won't take long, hot watah and coal."

Slocum went into the small bathroom and gingerly peeled off his shirt. He felt strips sticking to his wounds. That had to come off in the bath. After he hung up his six-shooter on a clothes hook, he sat on the edge of the bathtub and worked off his boots. Wiggling his toes felt good. He looked up when Jefferson came into the room with two large buckets.

"This heah watah's pipin' hot aw'ready. Got it from the Bullet's boiler. You be careful gettin' in. I got more watah heatin' on the stove."

Jefferson sloshed plenty of water in. Steam rose. Just holding his hand in the rising heat soothed Slocum. Before he shucked off his pants, he grabbed a bar of soap and sniffed at it. Ladies' perfumed soap would make him stink to high heaven. Somehow, he didn't care what Jefferson or Mad Tom or any of the other crew thought about that. The memory of being clean was so distant he would gladly trade a bit of stinkum for that feeling again.

He stepped into the water. It stung but he plunged on in. The hot water burned the spot on his leg where Big Joe had shot him. He peeled off the bandage and tossed it aside, then slowly lowered himself in the water. It sloshed about but didn't go over the sides. The tub proved larger than he had thought. He couldn't quite stretch out his long legs, but sitting up, his back against the tall end, let him relax. He closed his eyes and began to drift off to sleep. Slocum came awake with a start when the soap slipped from his hand.

"I'll get it for you."

He jerked around as a hand plunged under the water hunting for the soap and found something more. The fingers stroked along his thigh, his inner thigh, then a tad higher until they danced over his privates.

"There's no need to be so tense," Sarah Jane said. "I do this all the time. I'm quite expert." Her fingers stroked over him, circled him, began to gently squeeze until he hardened under her erotic aggression.

"Do you do this for Morgan Burlison?"

Sarah Jane jerked back and angrily spat like a wet cat. Before she could protest, Slocum grabbed her arms and pulled her back to the side of the tub to give her a long, hard kiss. She fought a few seconds, then melted. Her kiss turned into an amazing dance of her tongue slipping and sliding past his, dueling and teasing.

"I want that kind of motion," she said breathlessly. "But down lower and with this." She grabbed hold of his organ and stroked vigorously.

Slocum didn't think he could get much harder, but he did just by thinking about possessing this wicked, wild woman. Hands wet and fingers slippery with soap, he worked to get her blouse open. Her breasts tumbled out, naked and free. They bobbed just enough to entice him to bend lower. The water in the tub sloshed out onto the floor, but he didn't care. All he could see were those two creamy globes capped with brownish nips. As he sucked one of those fleshy caps between his lips, he felt the hammering of her heart. He pressed down with his tongue as he increased suction.

She arched her back, trying to jam her entire tit into his mouth. He denied her. Running his tongue about in a spiral, he slipped down one slope and worked his way up the other to repeat his licking and teasing.

"You like that, don't you?"

"I want more. I told you. I'm wet. For you."

"I know," Slocum said. He slipped around in the tub and pulled her in so she straddled his legs.

His hands reluctantly stopped stroking over her chest and worked lower, pushing up under her clinging wet skirt. He found her trembling thigh. Squeezing and pinching lightly brought her to labored gasps. She almost passed out when his thumb slipped upward through the lush garden of her bush and into her innermost reaches. He gripped down around her leg with his fingers as he moved the thumb in and out. Strong inner muscles tried to clamp down on him, to hold him, to get the most possible excitement imaginable from his hand. But his thumb was too small.

He moved out of her oily interior and hiked her skirts even higher until they rolled about her waist so her privates were fully exposed.

"If you like what you see, what are you going to do about it?"

He lightly swatted her behind, then grabbed a handful of luscious ass flesh and maneuvered her so she was poised directly over the head of his throbbing manhood. Without a word, he pushed down on her hips. She tried to resist, playfully wanting more. Slocum found his need too great for more foreplay. After all he had been through, he needed her.

He twisted her from side to side until she lowered her hips. He gasped as his thick head pressed between her pink lips and then plunged balls deep into her heated core. For a moment, they remained still, unable to do anything but let the sensations pound through them. Then Sarah Jane moved.

Slowly she lifted herself. Slocum guided her and then slid his hands up her sides and cupped both breasts. Catching the nipples between his thumbs and forefingers, he twisted and turned. She moaned softly and tried to follow the directions he moved her body. Then he pulled downward.

Once more she engulfed him. His shaft jerked hard within the tight female sheath. Then it got even tighter. He had gotten a hint of how strong her inner muscles were when his thumb had been diddling her. Now she squeezed powerfully until he thought he was in a virgin. He abandoned his post on her tits and once more roved her sleek body. This time his thumb stopped at the top of the vee just above where he disappeared into her. Pressing down here produced a skyrocket effect in her.

Sarah Jane arched her back, jammed her hips down even harder into his groin, and let out a long, loud shriek of carnal release. He felt her shudder and settle back down, but he was nowhere near through with her. His finger parted her fleshy half-moons and probed until he found another hole to enter. This caused her to rise. He controlled her perfectly by how he rammed in and out of her back.

Faster and faster he sent her rising and falling. The water had long since sloshed out of the tub. What remained evaporated and chilled his flesh. The contrast between her fiery innards and the coldness of his legs and midriff spurred him on until he felt fire ignite deep within his loins. The white-hot tide rose along his length, and as Sarah Jane pumped up and down in a passion, he exploded. He pulled her chest to his face and buried himself between her boobs. His arms circled her and held her tight, to keep her in place, to prevent her from slipping away as he spurted powerfully.

Only when he began to melt within her did he release the woman so she could rock back and look at him. Her face flushed and her skin rosy all the way down to the tops of her breasts, she eyed him like a hungry wolf did a rabbit.

"I knew you were something special, John. It's never been this good."

"Might be you learned a thing or two spying on that gent back in the whorehouse."

"I knew all about that before. I only wanted to see if he did anything different—or she did."

"She was a professional, after all," Slocum said. He idly stroked over her body, occasionally flicking his thumb against a nip. The blood was retreating now that her passion faded, but she still appreciated the attention. When he tried to move on, she clamped both of her hands over his and pressed down until he felt the soft flesh compress.

"More," she said in a husky voice. "I want more."

"So do I," he said. She grinned just like that wolf, then turned mad when he said, "I want more hot water for my bath. Go fetch it."

Sarah Jane sputtered, then pushed herself to a seat on the edge of the tub. Scissoring her legs so she lifted first one and then the other over his head to give him one last look at the paradise where he had been, she got to her feet and wetly padded out. He heard the car door slam. Slocum leaned back in the tub, then got out himself. He had water to heat and a proper bath to take before he put on the fancy duds Burlison had given him.

If the rest of the trip to Texas rivaled the way it had started, he was ready for it—and seeing more of Sarah Jane along the way.

6

The Yuma Bullet lived up to its name as it pulled away from the San Diego yards. Slocum had felt a mite uncomfortable wearing Burlison's hand-me-downs, especially so when he had shaken the railroad officer's hand for the last time before their trains went in different directions. Burlison had chugged away to his meeting in San Francisco and the short train carrying his daughter finally steamed past the spot where the rail had been removed and burst out into the arid countryside.

Slocum stared out the window of his Pullman car. Marlene and her sexy maid were holed up in the first car. Even over the clanking of the steel wheels, he heard snippets of an argument. If he had been more interested, he would have spied on them the way Jefferson did. The conductor stood on the narrow platform between cars, making no bones about eavesdropping. When the dry wind began blowing off the hard desert, the conductor came back into Slocum's car and looked around.

"You shore do live like a king heah," the conductor said.

"First time for everything," Slocum said. He had found

a small bar and had poured himself three shots of whiskey. Holding up the glass, he silently offered one to the man. Jefferson shook his head.

"Not whilst I on duty."

"What are they arguing about?" Slocum's eyes darted toward the front of the train.

"You cain't figger that out? You smarter 'n that, Slocum."

Sipping the whiskey relieved some of the aches and pains he had accumulated in San Diego and while repairing the engine. The bath had cleaned out the scrapes and cuts and Sarah Jane had done her best to make him forget the worst of his injuries. For her part, she had succeeded better than the fine whiskey.

"That's a strange pair," he said.

"They don't look so strange to me, but what do I know? I's only a po' black fella who don't git to look on no nekkid white lady. That ain't what's evah gonna happen."

Slocum laughed. "I meant Marlene and Sarah Jane, not Sarah Jane's, uh, endowments. It hardly seems Sarah Jane works for the boss's daughter the way she acts."

"She do be a quiet one."

"You've got quite a sense of humor. The pair of them were in a cathouse and Sarah Jane was watching a man take one of the soiled doves like she was a dog. Spying on them through a peephole in the wall."

"Do tell. Sarah Jane's got mo' to her than I'da thunk." Jefferson checked his watch, studied it as if the secrets of the universe were revealed, then snapped shut the lid and replaced the gold watch in a vest pocket. "We's 'bout ready to cross the ribber."

"You sound worried. Should I be?"

"That there trestle's been mighty shaky ever' time we rolled ovah it. We don't get ovah that bridge, we don't go nowheah."

Slocum downed his whiskey and let it warm him. He couldn't help comparing this warmth with what Sarah Jane had sparked inside him. That was better. Climbing to his feet, he stretched. Seams across the coat's shoulders gave way. Slocum was broader there than Burlison and the shirt flapped around his chest and middle. Burlison carried greater girth than did Slocum, but the fine cloth felt as good as anything he'd ever worn, other than Sarah Jane, in a long time. The clothing was expensive and gave him the look of a man of means, even if he didn't have two dimes to rub together.

He settled his six-shooter at his hip and followed Jefferson forward. Since the train had pulled out, he hadn't budged from his car. If he wanted to talk to Mad Tom, he had to pass through Marlene's car—and get another look at Sarah Jane.

The car had been partitioned so there were two sleeping quarters. Marlene sat on a chair in the common area working on needlepoint. When Slocum and Jefferson entered the car, she looked up and smiled. Slocum recognized the expression and wasn't about to do anything about it. She was the boss's daughter. Besides, he had a spitfire in Sarah Jane to keep him company whenever she could sneak away from her mistress.

"Good day, Mr. Slocum."

"Ma'am," Slocum said, touching the brim of his hat.

"You folk, now, you do go on and settle mattahs." Jefferson disappeared through the front door and worked his way outside along the tender to talk to Mad Tom.

"I should go, too," Slocum said, but a strange reluctance to leave held him as if his boots had been glued to the floor.

He glanced down at a table where a book was laid facedown.

"Do you know Mark Twain, Mr. Slocum? That is his newest title. It hasn't been published in this country yet. That is a Canadian edition."

"Sounds like me."

"I beg your pardon?"

Slocum tapped the book. "*The Prince and the Pauper.* I'm a pauper all duded up in your pa's finest."

"There needs to be some tailoring done. I will be happy to do it if you let me take your measure." Marlene blushed and looked away. "That didn't come out the way I'd intended."

"Where's Miss Mulligan?"

"Why, I . . . she was feeling poorly and is taking a nap. The heat, you know. It is brutal and will only get worse when we cross the river."

"Past Yuma gets mighty hot this time of year," Slocum said. "It's kind of you to let your maid sleep like this."

"There's nothing to do or see along this stretch of the line." A ghost of a smile flickered across her lips. "What else could I do to pass the time?"

"You could read the book," Slocum said, glancing in the direction of the Twain novel.

"I suppose I could. I'd rather work to get that coat of yours to fit properly." She stood, then stumbled when the train suddenly braked, falling into Slocum's arms.

Slocum caught her. She fit into the circle of his arms nicely. He took a deep breath and caught the faint gardenia scent of her perfume. She looked up, her eyes wider than normal, then pushed away from him and tried to smooth out the wrinkles in her skirts.

"Why did we come to a halt?" Sarah Jane came from the larger of the two sleeping quarters, her dark hair mussed and her eyes bleary. "We can't be in Yuma yet to take on water and coal."

"I'll check," Slocum said, his hands lingering on Marlene's waist. He picked her up and spun her about. She was as light as a feather.

"Hurry, John. I don't like my sleep being disturbed like this."

"Now, Miss Mulligan, don't be rude," Marlene said.

For an instant fire passed between the two, then died.

"I'm sorry. Hurry along, John. Find out why that foolish

crazy-eyed engineer brought us to a halt." Sarah Jane looked out the window at the desolate landscape.

Slocum opened the front door and stepped into the hot wind. He caught at his hat to keep it from flying off as he swung around and found the ledge along the tender's outer wall that led forward to the cab. The land wasn't as much a desert as he had thought looking from Marlene's Pullman car. The vegetation ahead turned lush as it dropped down toward the Colorado River. Without the clacking of wheels against the tracks, he heard the rush of the powerful river.

As he edged along, he saw a curious sight ahead along the tracks. A rainbow arched above the trestle. The river threw up a constant mist that made it seem as if the train would be running under the rainbow. But in this desert, the real pot of gold at either end of the rainbow had to be the water in the river fifty feet below.

Jefferson and Mad Tom stood toe to toe, arguing, when Slocum stepped into the cab. The fireman sat silently on a drop seat near the closed iron grate that opened to the boiler. He smiled, a white gash in a face filthy with coal dust. Rocking back, crossing his legs, he folded his arms on his chest and enjoyed the spectacle of the engineer and conductor fighting.

"What's wrong?" Slocum asked.

The two men turned on him.

"I ain't pushin' the Bullet 'cross the bridge 'less them fools say it's safe," Mad Tom said.

"They only workmen, not engineerahs," Jefferson said.

Slocum saw that four men had gathered along the tracks. They leaned on pry bars and shovel handles. The engineer and conductor went back to their argument. Slocum climbed down and went to the crew.

"Why do you have the lanterns up?" He pointed at the two lanterns hung from poles swaying in the wind. The glass had been painted red to give a warning.

"Well, sir, it's like this," said the one that Slocum took

to be the foreman. "There was a powerful wind last night that sent a big wave racin' down the river. Struck the far support just 'fore dawn. Me and the boys are tryin' to figger out if it's safe for a train to go across."

"The bridge might collapse?"

"Might not either," the foreman said. "Without climbin' down and doin' a complete examination, can't say one way or the other."

"Have you seen damage happen to a bridge from such currents before?"

The foreman spat, wiped his mouth, and silently nodded.

"How long will it take for you to check out the supports?"

"Can't rightly say. Might be a day 'fore we can climb down. Real dangerous since the wood gets all wet and slippery."

Slocum walked to the edge of the cliff and looked down into the roiling, raging Colorado. The bridge supports looked secure, but he wasn't an expert. He jerked around when the foreman touched his arm and held out field glasses.

"What am I looking for?"

"Signs of damage, maybe the wood being chewed away like some damn animal's hungry for it."

Slocum studied the nearer bridge supports, then worked to the far ones on the east side of the river. He moved a few yards and got a better angle. He handed back the glasses.

"The far timbers look bowed."

"Not supposed to be that way. I have to run my hands over the wood to get a feel for how safe it is if there's nuthin' showin' up more 'n bowed supports," the foreman said. "Replacing those struts would take a week, once we get the timber."

"I'll tell the engineer," Slocum said. He walked slowly back to the Yuma Bullet, where Jefferson and Mad Tom had run out of words and stood facing away from each other, arms crossed and looking fierce.

"The bridge supports might be shaky," Slocum said.

"They don't know what they talkin' 'bout. We got to move on along," Jefferson said. "Theah's a schedule to keep." He took his watch from his vest pocket and made a big show of studying it.

"I ain't riskin' *my* train goin' over a bad bridge. This here trestle's been a caution since it was built."

"Mr. Burlison'd want us to go on."

Slocum looked at the conductor and finally said, "Even if it means risking the life of his daughter?"

"He knowed the condition of the road. He ain't nobody's fool," Jefferson said. "It's *his* road."

"The river just rose last night and shook the foundations this morning." Slocum looked across the bridge. The mist still rose from the river, but the sun had sunk low enough behind them to erase the rainbow. "Why not wait for a train coming from Yuma going to San Diego and see how it fares?"

"We ain't got a siding heah, Mistah Slocum. How we s'pposed to let the train by?"

"He's got a point," Mad Tom said. "We'd have to back up danged near twenty miles to find a siding. Railroad schedules are precise." He walked forward, chewing on his lower lip. Finally he came to a decision. "If the work crew thinks we kin make it, we go. They say no, we wait. Don't care if we have to back up all the way to the Pacific Ocean."

Slocum hollered and got the repair crew foreman over.

"You boys decide on what to do?" the foreman asked.

"That depends on your expert opinion," Slocum said. "The trestle is upright but bowed. You didn't see any damage that would let you put a bet on a train taking a dive into the river?"

"Ain't a bettin' man, but I see what you're askin'." He scratched himself, shuffled about, and finally said, "Without climbin' down, ain't no way to say if it's safe. I got me a man workin' his way down now." He took his field glasses and walked to the lip of the cliff. After several seconds, he lowered them. "Either Ray's wavin' you on or he's got a foot stuck."

"Then he's wavin' us on," Mad Tom said. "Get to stokin', you useless piece of shit." He swung into the cab. The fireman had already shoveled coal into the boiler to build up a head of steam to cross.

Jefferson grinned and slapped Slocum on the back.

"We's gonna be in Yuma by mornin'. Take some time, git a good breakfast." He cupped his hands to his mouth and bellowed, "All aboard! We's pullin' out!"

Slocum looked across the twilight-shrouded tracks. He had never crossed the river on a train and had no idea what a bridge looked like, but this one seemed to sway. Mad Tom leaned out the side of the cab, yanked on the whistle lanyard, and released the brakes. The Yuma Bullet edged forward.

"You gonna be left behind if you don't climb aboard, Slocum," the engineer said.

Slocum waved and let the tender pass before he hopped up on the platform leading into Marlene's car. The locomotive reached the western side of the bridge. Mad Tom advanced carefully, as if testing the bridge. Then he let loose with another loud whistle and the train picked up speed. Slocum appreciated that. The faster they went, the sooner they'd reach safety on the eastern side.

He opened the door and went in. Sarah Jane sat where Marlene had been earlier. She gripped the arms of the chair. Her blue eyes widened in fear.

"The bridge is wobbling," she said in a tiny voice.

"It's all right, Sarah Jane," Slocum said. "Where're Miss Burlison and Jefferson?"

"The next car. I think they were going to the mail car. Don't worry about them. Stay with me. I'm frightened!"

Slocum ignored her plea, took a step toward the rear of the car, and lost his balance. He slammed hard into the side, his elbow breaking a window. Catching himself, he reached up and started to pull the emergency cord that signaled the engineer to halt. The Yuma Bullet plowed on ahead. Another whistle blast about deafened him. This one came long and loud.

"Are we going up a hill?" Sarah Jane asked. "What's happening? Tell me, dammit!"

Slocum looked toward the rear of the car. It ran downward at an increasing angle.

"The bridge is giving way!"

"Don't leave me. They're able to take care of themselves. Save me, John. You have to stay with *me!*" Sarah Jane staggered to him and clung fiercely. "Don't go back *there!*"

"Get into the engine cab. Run!" Slocum shoved a screaming Sarah Jane up the slope to the front door and shoved her through it into the next car.

All he had to do to get to the rear of the Pullman was to relax and let gravity pull him. He flung open the rear door. Wood creaked and snapped. The train slewed to one side, righted itself, then began sliding away backward. Mad Tom applied all the power locked in the Yuma Bullet and for a moment Slocum thought it would be enough.

Marlene Burlison reached the door from the second Pullman car. Sheer panic etched her lovely features. She screamed but the cry disappeared amid the sounds of wood snapping and steel twisting.

"Grab hold!" Slocum yelled. He leaned over the railing on the platform and held out his hand. All she had to do was open the door and take his hand.

He watched in horror as the Pullman car detached from the coupling, then plunged into the darkness. Amid the pounding of pistons, the hiss of steam, and the roar of the river below, he heard a loud splash as the sleeping car with Marlene inside crashed into the water.

7

Slocum almost followed Marlene down as the train lurched. The incline disappeared as the train righted itself and the speed increased, taking the Yuma Bullet away from the collapsed portion of the bridge and onto solid ground. He hung on, watching the deadly spot on the tracks vanish into the dark. He shoved himself to his feet and ran through the Pullman car to the front door, where he plowed into Sarah Jane, knocking her to one side.

"John, what happened?"

"The last three cars fell into the river," he said.

Sarah Jane turned white and swayed. Slocum caught her as she swooned, then he whirled her about and put her into one of the chairs that had wedged itself near the door.

"Wait, where are you going?" Her words came out weak and frightened. "Don't leave me! I'm ordering you. Don't leave me!"

Slocum hesitated. That wasn't what he'd expected from the woman. Her life was one of service and toil, yet her first thought was for herself. Marlene might not be an easy mistress, but Slocum expected more from Sarah Jane than this self-centered arrogance.

"I have to stop the train first," he said.

Slocum made his way forward to where the fireman shoveled furiously and Mad Tom leaned into the lever controlling the speed looking every bit the maniac of his moniker. The engineer's brawny wrist flexed as Slocum grabbed it to pull back on the throttle.

"The last three cars are gone," Slocum said. "Stop the train. Now!"

"Lost?" Mad Tom had been dazed and reacting out of shock. He jerked free and pulled back slowly on the throttle before applying the brakes. He cursed at the fireman to stop stoking. When the Yuma Bullet stopped, he stared hard at Slocum.

The flickering orange light from the boiler's flames turned the engineer into something eerie and evil.

"The bridge went out under the rear of the train," Slocum said. "Miss Burlison's car is the only one you have left."

"The caboose, mail car, and second Pullman? Gone?"

"Miss Burlison was in the second Pullman when it went into the river," Slocum said. He looked around, then turned cold inside. "Jefferson must have been with her."

"He's not with Sarah Jane?"

"I'm afraid not," Slocum said. He hoped Mad Tom got his wits back. "How far until you reach Yuma and get help? You have to warn westbound trains that the bridge is out."

"The repair crew is on the other side," Mad Tom said dully. "They can get word to San Diego."

"And you can go ahead and tell them in Yuma what the trouble is."

"The bridge," Mad Tom said. He perked up. "You said Miss Burlison's maid is all right?"

"Shaken up, but she's not harmed." Slocum swung out, hanging on to a handrail, and looked back toward the Colorado. The river's roar could be heard, but there wasn't any sign the bridge had collapsed. In the dark that could be deadly for another train. "Mark the tracks as dangerous so another train won't go into the drink."

"We're on the only track. Nuthin' can pass us," the fireman said.

Slocum was glad one of them was thinking clearly. He obviously wasn't because he was worried about something that couldn't happen.

"I'll see what I can take with me to rescue Miss Burlison," he said.

"Ain't much in that there sleepin' car," Mad Tom said. "No rope or food or much o' anything."

"Get moving. Send back a repair party for me as quick as you can."

Slocum jumped to the ground. He looked up and saw Mad Tom staring ahead as if he saw through the darkness. Without a word, the engineer took off the brakes and the locomotive began chugging forward. In seconds the Pullman car swept past Slocum. Sarah Jane pressed into the window, waved to him, and shouted something he couldn't hear over the ruckus. In less than a minute the Yuma Bullet rattled into the night out of sight.

He hitched up his gun belt and began the hike back to the bridge. Every step might have been one more up to the gallows for his own hanging. When he reached the black chasm filled with the roaring Colorado River, he simply stared. The bridge had collapsed three-quarters of the way across. Twisted tracks showed how the Yuma Bullet had powered itself forward at the expense of the last three cars.

Edging along carefully, he found a spar that had been ripped free on one end but remained fixed at the other. Slocum grabbed hold and worked his way out until his feet dangled down. Hanging by his hands, he judged distances and finally dropped. He fell twenty feet, hit the cross beam he had expected, only the impact proved too great. His legs collapsed under him. Plunging outward, he screamed. The mocking echo was swallowed by the river's rush. When he was sure he would follow the railroad cars into the current, another cross beam smashed into his chest, spinning him upright.

More from blind luck than skill, he grabbed on to the slippery wooden joist and swung back and forth. He hiked up one foot, caught the top of the beam, and pulled himself flat. He lay prone on the beam gasping for breath. A mule had kicked him in the chest once. The obnoxious animal's hoof hadn't hurt any more than the impact with the beam. As good as it felt to simply lie still, he forced himself to hands and knees and crept along until he came to an upright support.

The work crew had nailed short crosspieces on it to use as a ladder. Looking up, he saw that direction went nowhere. This was where the trestle had given way under the weight of the train. Stars littered the sky but gave little illumination as he gripped the first rung and tested it. Lowering his foot located another and another.

The only evidence that he was headed in the right direction in the darkness came from the increasing mist sprayed upward. Ten minutes of working his way down the crude ladder brought him to the supports driven into the rocky riverbank. He stepped away and sat on a rock, trying to make out details in the river.

Wagon trains had likely forded the Colorado here. The mail car had fallen rear wall down and was mired in a sandbank.

"Hullo!" His call and the roar of the river mingled and turned into nothing but noise. The mail clerk might still be alive inside. Or Jefferson. Or Marlene Burlison.

Slocum hunted about and found pieces of broken railcar along the bank. From the evidence, at least one of the cars had fallen into the rocks before being bounced into the river and swept away. He found two sturdy planks. Taking off his coat, he ran the wood through the sleeves to make a raft.

Gauging the river's speed, he walked a hundred yards upriver. Not sure he would survive but having to look, he took a run at the water and thrust out the raft before him. Water surged about him and kicked up white foam when he hit belly down. For an instant undertow submerged him but he clung fiercely to the coat holding the wood planks in place. He bobbed to the surface, half lying on the raft.

The current swept him toward the sandbar. Kicking hard and not trying to go against the current, he angled toward the mail car. He misjudged distances and smashed hard into an axle poking out of the sand. A quick grab secured his position and kept him from washing away. Slocum got his feet under him but still had to cling to the axle for balance. Carefully moving, he got around the side of the mail car. Fully half of it had been buried when it came crashing down, but the door had popped free, leaving a way inside.

"Jefferson? You in there? Marlene?" He didn't know the mail clerk's name, but if the man heard him calling for the others, he would respond.

Hearing nothing, Slocum pulled himself up over the edge of the open door. Whatever had been in the safe was gone for good. The fall had ripped the iron safe from where it had been bolted to the floor and the river had carried it away. A huge hole in what had been the car roof showed where the safe had gone.

An arm poked out from under a pile of mailbags. Slocum scrambled over and began throwing the bags off until he found the mail clerk. He shouldn't have bothered. The mailbags had been a more fitting grave for the man than the spray kicked up by the river. The man's head hung at an unnatural angle, showing how he had died. The only consolation Slocum could find was that the death had been quick.

A more thorough search of what remained of the car turned up no trace of either Marlene or Jefferson. He worked his way up and came out on the upside of the car. Looking downstream caused his heart to race. The Pullman car hadn't washed away but had beached a couple hundred feet away. If he hadn't been so intent on the river directly under the bridge, he would have seen it while he clung to the trestle.

He found his coat-raft and launched himself once more, heading for the Pullman car. He feared the depth of the river might cause undertow but a rocky outjut produced a shallow pool. He whipped around, got caught in the pool, and slammed into the shoreline. The protection afforded by the rocks kept the current from pulling him back into the river.

Aching and banged up, he dragged himself farther up the shore. He wanted to rush over to examine the Pullman car, but all his strength had been sucked out of his body by the harsh current and cold water. It rankled but he forced himself to rest. Only then did he call out to draw the attention of any survivor.

No answer to his shout.

Slocum walked over the slippery rocks and got to the car. It lay with the roof against the canyon wall, its undercarriage out into the river. At what had once been the front of the car, he tried to open the door. Stuck. Then a faint cry from inside spurred him on. He put one boot against the wall and grabbed with both hands, heaving hard. The door flew out of the frame.

"Mr. Slocum," came the weak cry. "Help me."

He made his way into the pitch-black interior. The lamps had all burned out. The impact had ruptured the tanks holding the gas. If it hadn't been for the sudden immersion in the river, there might have been a fire.

"I'm coming," he said, working past an overturned couch. Then he stopped. His foot went down into something yielding.

He swung to one side and used his feet to push away the couch. Even in the darkness he knew a dead body from a living one. The conductor had died. It hardly mattered if it came from the fall or drowning or something else. Jefferson was very dead.

"Where are you?"

"Here, John. I can't move my legs. Help me!"

He threw aside furniture and other debris to reach the woman. She lay in a heap, her blond hair masking her face. Her clothing had been ripped in a dozen places. Both legs were pinned by a section of the Pullman car wall that had been smashed inward.

"This will take a couple minutes. Can you feel your legs?" He reached down and ran his hand along her leg all the way to her inner thigh.

"Sir, please!"

He laughed. "You felt that?"

"I did, sir!"

"Then your legs aren't paralyzed. I've seen that happen during the war. One of my men was sitting under a tree when a Yankee cannonball crashed through the trunk. A tree fell over and a heavy limb fell on his legs."

As he talked to keep her occupied, he found a grip on the wood.

"What happened to him?"

"He never walked again."

"No!"

Slocum grunted and exerted all his strength to lift the wood away. Marlene rolled onto her side and got out from under it an instant before he slipped and let the wood crash back down. He sat back and looked at her.

"You have a terrible way of telling stories, Mr. Slocum."

"You're going to be just fine. I see how you're kicking up your heels."

"Really!" Marlene sat up and straightened her legs, then brought her knees up and moved them about. "I am free. Thank you. But that story was terrible, of the man who became paralyzed."

"He wasn't paralyzed," Slocum said, standing. He offered her his hand, then pulled her to her feet. She stood without any difficulty. "He died."

"Then why did you say—"

"Didn't want to worry you none."

He teetered when the entire car began to slide back toward the river.

"We must get free immediately," Marlene said. "Do you need help?"

The question startled him. She held out her hand to steady him because he had lost his balance and sat down heavily when the car's weight shifted.

"I'm fine," he said. As he followed her, he started noticing how her clothes hung in revealing tatters. "Are there any clothes in this car you can wear?"

"Why, yes, I suppose all of them would fit. Oh!" She realized why he had asked. Her left breast was exposed as was her left leg all the way from ankle to hip. "I didn't realize I was indecent."

Slocum wondered at this. Here was a woman who took her maid to a whorehouse to spy on a man and woman in the next room, yet dishevelment after falling down into the Colorado River embarrassed her.

"There's a wardrobe. Is it Sarah Jane's?" He heaved open a door to a wardrobe tipped on its side. "Better hurry." The car slipped a bit more as the current caught part of it and sought to suck it into the flow.

"I always liked this dress, but it isn't suitable for what we must do to get out. Here, yes, this will do." She grabbed several items and clung to them as he herded her out of the car.

The screeching of wood dragged across rock drowned out conversation for a few seconds. Then the Pullman car spun out into the river, where the rapid current tore it in half as if it were nothing but tissue paper.

"Such power in that river," Marlene said as they watched

from the bank. "Thank you for saving me. I could have been killed."

"We all could have been killed." He looked up at the sheer wall of black, slippery stone. Returning to the rim would take some doing.

"What of the others? Jefferson is gone. I saw him die and could do nothing to help him."

"The mail clerk's a goner, too."

"What of . . . of Sarah Jane? She is all right?" Real concern gave a poignant ring to her words that again surprised Slocum. She truly cared for her maid and wanted to know her fate.

"She's on the way to Yuma. Mad Tom is highballing it to let them know to send out a repair crew. If the crew we met on the western side is on the ball, the bridge can be repaired in two shakes of a lamb's tail."

"How are we going to get to the top?" Marlene looked up at the unscalable wall. "I'm sure you have a plan. You're very capable."

"There is a set of rungs hammered onto the bridge support. We can use that to climb almost to the top."

"Almost?"

"We'll cross that bridge when we get to it," he said. He laughed ruefully. "Even if we didn't do much of a job crossing it the first time."

"Your outlook on the world is very strange, Mr. Slocum. Now please turn your back so I can change."

He let her strip off her damaged clothes and work into the duds she had taken from the car. While she dressed, he hiked back toward the bridge supports. The construction crew had cleared a path, making it easier to reach the spot where the rung ladder climbed up the support.

"I see where the trestle crumpled," Marlene said. She pressed close to him. Although she had changed into decent clothing, she was as soaked through as he was from the constant spray. A little shiver hinted at how cold she was but she never complained. "Is that the way to the top of the world?"

"Back to the world," Slocum said. He looked at her. Starlight caught water droplets in her hair and turned them into diamonds amid the golden strands. Although she was drenched and shivered like a drowning rat, he found himself liking the way she looked. It was natural and wild.

Slocum shook himself. This wasn't the time, and she was the boss's daughter.

"Should I go first or will you?"

"If I followed, I'd be forced to look up your skirt the whole way," he said.

Marlene recoiled, then grinned a little. "Is that such a burden for you, Mr. Slocum?"

"If it doesn't offend you, your going first makes sense. My heavier weight might pull loose a rung. You'd never be able to keep me from toppling into the river."

"But my lighter weight might not dislodge a loose rung? Yes, that makes sense. And if I fell, you could rescue me. Very well. I'll go first."

Slocum marveled that she believed he could catch her if she fell, yet he detected no hint of sarcasm in her words. She began climbing. When he followed, he discovered that the darkness prevented him from seeing anything that would offend her modesty.

"It is a very long way to the top, isn't it?" she called back after fifteen minutes of climbing.

"Rest if you have to. We can find a cross beam and sit on that."

"I was not complaining, just opining that it is taking so long. Why, the sky is brightening. Dawn cannot be far away."

Slocum tried to piece together how long he had taken from the time he jumped off the Yuma Bullet to now. It all flowed together like the river below. Jefferson and the mail clerk were dead and lost in watery graves, but he had saved Marlene Burlison. Or had he really? Her legs had been pinned but her spunk and determination told him she wouldn't have simply given up and died. Somehow she would have saved herself. That presence of mind appealed to him.

"I see the top! I do!"

She scrambled up the rungs faster now, giving Slocum a better look at her legs. The faint dawn helped. And once she had reached the tracks, she was bathed in the warmth of a new desert day.

Slocum pulled himself up after her, then froze.

"They haven't come to rescue us, have they?" Marlene said in a low voice.

Slocum looked at the Apache braves decked out in their war paint. The Indians turned their horses toward him and began trotting over, waving rifles in the air.

"No, they haven't."

8

Slocum stepped forward and put himself between the Indians and Marlene. The riders came hard, kicking up a dust cloud that obscured the railroad tracks. With a lightning-fast calculation, Slocum realized the Apaches might not have seen Marlene. He stepped back, grabbed her around the waist, and picked her up, kicking.

"What are you doing, Mr. Slocum? Put me down."

He did. He dropped her between the cross ties to a rocky slope beneath. Marlene yelped and lost her footing. For a frightening instant he thought she would tumble on down the side of the canyon and fall back into the river. An agile twist brought her around to slide on her belly. She found purchase with her toes and then seized a ragged hunk of metal sticking down from the tracks.

"Don't say a word. Don't move," he ordered as he slid his Colt from its holster. The water trickling from the barrel told him there wasn't a chance in hell the pistol would fire. The repeated dips in the river had ruined the cartridges and possibly gummed up the firing mechanism. He slid it back into its holster and looked for other ways to fight.

"Don't leave me here. I can help you," protested the woman. She scrambled up so there was no chance of falling over the cliff face into the river.

Slocum picked up a discarded sledgehammer handle. It had broken and been cast away. He swung it a couple times. Its heft was gone with the steel head but the sharp point where the wood had splintered promised a spear thrust if he got close enough to use it that way.

The dust cleared and four warriors drew rein twenty feet away. They whooped and hollered as they waved their rifles in the air. Slocum stood his ground, sledgehammer handle ready to swing. He couldn't help looking down under the tracks to where Marlene huddled. A touch of admiration came. She hid but wasn't frightened. Then the admiration faded when he realized she had no idea what they faced. A woman living in the lap of luxury had never confronted Indians who would kill her and lift her scalp—or worse, take her prisoner. A pretty woman could be used for weeks before they killed her. Since this was a war party, however, Slocum doubted Marlene would be given even a week.

They would use her, then kill her right away. That might be merciful. It was better she avoid it entirely, even if he had to die defending her. Given enough time, Mad Tom would report the bridge collapse and the S&P would send back a repair crew. The workers on the western side might have telegraphed the problem in both directions—east and west—already. If so, help might only be minutes away.

Slocum had to make a decision right now.

The youngest of the braves lowered his rifle and raked his moccasins along his pony's flanks. The war chief let the youth attack to gain experience and honor in combat. Slocum denied him both.

As the Apache galloped down, Slocum stepped sideways so the Indian had to reach across his body with his rifle, ruining his ability to fire accurately. Rather than using his wooden handle on the rider, Slocum swung it hard and connected with the horse's left front leg. The horse stumbled from the blow and sent the Apache flying.

Immediately pressing the fight, Slocum used the sharp-tipped handle to stab the fallen rider. The broken splinter sank into the man's right shoulder. Slocum leaned hard on it as the Apache writhed about. The agonized shriek brought the other three warriors galloping down on him. Twisting the handle, Slocum inflicted enough pain that the fallen Indian passed out.

Scooping up the man's rifle, Slocum got off three fast shots. All missed but they forced his attackers to veer away. He could have taken more accurate aim and shot one of the retreating Indians from horseback. Instead he went after the downed brave's horse.

The animal tried to rear, but Slocum had to get away from this spot. He pulled down the horse's head, then vaulted onto the pony's back. Giving the horse its head caused him to race away after the other three. As he thundered above her, Slocum waved for Marlene to stay low. She yelled something, but he raced past too fast to understand.

When he got onto solid ground, he veered away from the others, using the dust cloud to mask his real direction. As he pounded along, he worried that the Apaches had spotted Marlene, too. If he led them away and they didn't know she had been on the bridge, she had a good chance for survival. The S&P would have crews out right away to repair the bridge since it was their only route across the Colorado. The Union Pacific up north remained a transcontinental route, but other than this, the S&P had the only other one. Slocum had heard of others being built, but they all ran through New Mexico Territory and had to cross the Colorado River at some point.

The railroad crews would be especially alert because a vice president's daughter was part and parcel of the wreck. If she kept her head down, Marlene would be fine.

If Slocum successfully decoyed the Apaches away.

Bent down low, he chanced a look behind. Through the dust cloud came two riders. It meant death for him unless he got lucky, but Marlene was safe. He had done his job the best he could.

Slocum angled off, thinking to curve back toward the railroad tracks. What the Apaches sought other than his scalp was a poser since this stretch of desert was as barren as an old sow's womb. They must have escaped the reservation in the eastern part of Arizona and sought refuge here. Or they might have been chased to southwestern Arizona Territory by cavalry and looked to get across the border for the safety Mexico offered. Whatever the reason for the war party, the Apaches were intent on stopping Slocum.

That meant they feared he would reveal their position. Hope popped up a bit higher. Fort Barrett over on the Gila River was the closest military post. If these were Warm Springs Apaches off the reservation east of the fort, troopers might be close on their heels. All Slocum had to do was dodge about until the Indians began to worry about the soldiers finding them.

He crossed the railroad tracks and rode due north, but his pony began to flag. He slowed, alternated gaits, did what he could to keep moving without killing it under him. From the way his mouth filled with gummy cotton from lack of water, he knew the horse similarly suffered. The only sure source of water he knew in this desert roared along under the S&P bridge, but if he cut back in that direction, he risked Marlene being discovered.

Heading for low hills to the northwest, he had to slow almost to a walk. Even then the pony stumbled as it moved along. Slocum watched it closely for sign of ears pricking up or nostrils flaring at the scent of water. When nothing reached the horse, he knew he was in for tough times.

Canyons—hardly more than gullies—began to cut through the dry land. Slocum dropped to the ground, considered his chances, and then applied the flat of his hand to the horse's rump. It snorted, reared, and trotted away. Such a trick wouldn't slow the Apaches much, but getting the horse back as booty might satisfy them and they'd stop hunting for him.

The sun hammering down from directly above might wink out entirely, too. He knew false hope from reality. Choosing a ravine at random, he ran down it until his legs ached. The soft sand and hard pebbles robbed him of stamina and bruised his feet at the same time.

When a cutbank presented a hint of shade, he dived low and crawled out of the sun. Pressing his back against the crumbling sand wall, he took out his Colt Navy and examined it. The swim in the Colorado hadn't done it any good. Fearing the war party would come across him at any instant, he stripped the pistol and used the tail of the fancy shirt he had gotten from Burlison to wipe dry the metal parts. Without oil, he had to rely on metal grating against metal not to hang up from friction.

Each cartridge was carefully dried off and then slipped back into the cylinder. Whether any of the rounds would fire depended a great deal on how long they had been submerged. Slocum had dropped an entire box of cartridges into a river once, and after drying them off, all had fired. But the immersion had been only minutes. He tried to estimate the time he'd spent being slammed about in the Colorado and decided he couldn't. It all came to him as a soggy blur.

The sound of a horse coming from the east alerted him to danger. Slocum knew he could never get to the top of the bank and escape that way. He moved slowly, trying to stay in the shadows, retracing his path. The sound of the horse grew louder behind him. He slid his six-shooter from its holster and took careful aim at the bend in the ravine where an Apache rider had to appear.

The crushing weight on his shoulders, followed by a savage war whoop told him he had been tricked. Pressed facedown in the sand, he got nothing but dirt in his nose and mouth. A strong hand gripped his wrist, but he squeezed off a shot. It wouldn't have hit anyone, but he wanted an instant of surprise to give him an advantage.

The trap was too complete. Although the Indian atop him recoiled, two others dropped from the bank and held him down. One plucked the six-gun from his hand as another smashed him in the head with a rifle stock. He sagged, stunned. He shook his head and tried to focus. All he saw was a rider on a horse coming from the east. He tried to call out for help. Then his vision cleared enough to see that astride the unsaddled horse rode the war chief. He had been duped six ways to Sunday.

He was pulled to his feet and shoved about until his teeth rattled. Slocum knew what they did. If they kept him disoriented, it would be easier to make him talk.

But what could he possibly know that the Apaches would want?

A rawhide rope dropped over his head and tightened on his neck. Using the noose as a leash, a brave dragged him along. Slocum fought to keep up. The pace quickened when the brave vaulted onto his horse and started away at a brisk walk. If Slocum failed to keep up, he would be dragged through the desert by the rope around his neck.

Hanging on to it allowed him to keep a little slack and not get choked every time the Indian urged his horse to greater speed. Slocum struggled up sandy hills and down slopes that forced him to slide, but he never gave up. By the time they reached a camp, he thought the Apaches grudgingly afforded him some respect.

A snap on his leash forced him to his knees. The Indians spoke rapidly among themselves. He didn't speak their lingo but identified it as Tonto. They might have been put on the same reservation with the Warm Springs Apaches and other tribes from New Mexico, but this was their territory. If any cavalry troop sought them, it would be as hard as catching smoke. The Tonto knew every rise and valley from far up north down into Mexico.

The war chief came over, drew his knife, and laid the blade flat along Slocum's temple. A simple slash would take off an ear.

"How many?"

"What are you asking?" Slocum jerked away as the knife cut off part of his ear. He gagged as the rawhide rope tightened on his throat.

The Apache holding his rope kicked Slocum flat onto the ground.

"How many blue jackets come for us?"

Slocum knew they thought he was a cavalry scout. How he answered determined how long he would live. If he lied and said the cavalry was preparing to charge from over the nearest hill, he was a goner. They would cut his throat and ride away fast. Denying that he knew anything might convince them he was of no use, but they'd still kill him and ride away. If he pretended to know where the soldiers were but refused to tell, they would keep him alive so they could torture him for the information.

"The captain's looking for you," he said. Slocum cried out as the chief used the knife on his chest. Burlison's once fancy shirt had been soaked and dirtied and now sported a long, thin cut with blood welling up from the flesh beneath. "He'll take you back to the reservation. You won't like it any better this time."

"Are you a scout?"

Slocum nodded, then resolutely refused to say or do anything more. Hints. He had to tease them with hints that he knew more. How long he could endure their torture was another matter. The sun was well past noon and sinking fast in the direction of the Colorado River. Low hills separated them from the water. Focusing on the rush of water, he realized he had come in an almost full circle back to the bridge where he had left Marlene.

He screamed as the knife cut again.

"They'll be here soon enough. Riding on the railroad. Soldiers. Lots of them."

"You lie."

Slocum agreed that he was spinning a tall tale. The pain filled his body now. He would agree to anything the chief said.

"Soldiers come on horses. How far toward sunrise? How many days' ride?"

"Half a day," Slocum blurted out. It was the first answer that came to mind. He tried to keep his answers vague so they would let him live, but pain dulled his resolve. Closing his eyes, letting the warmth of the setting sun soothe him, he tried to push the pain away into a small dark corner of his mind. Denying it was impossible. If he could accept that he hurt—bad!—and tried to come up with plausible lies, he would stay alive a bit longer.

After another half hour of pain, he wondered why staying alive mattered. Death would be a relief after so many cuts. None was deep but all were painful. The chief knew the spots where his nerves protested the most from a shallow wound.

The chief stepped away and spoke at length. Two braves hurried to gather what weeds and branches from bushes they could for a fire. Another tended the horses. The other two drove stakes into the ground and fastened Slocum spread-eagle using lengths cut from the rawhide rope. When they soaked them in water from their cured hide desert bags, he knew a long night of agony awaited him.

As the water-soaked leather dried, it shrank. His arms and legs would slowly be pulled from his body. Starting the torture now when the sun was down meant the rawhide shrank more slowly. He had a night of pain ahead of him. If they had staked him out in the hot sun, the rawhide would have shrunk in minutes. Hours of being quartered lay ahead for him during the night.

Almost as tormenting was the smell of their cooking fires. Roasted rabbit made his mouth water and reminded him how long it had been since he'd had anything to eat. The good came with the bad. He was desperately thirsty, but the Indians had no intention of giving him water. The mouthwatering roasting meat was as close as he was going to get to a real drink.

The moon rose and cast its wan light on him. By now the cooking fire had died down and the Indians curled up under their blankets. Slocum shivered as the night took its revenge for such furnace-hot days. It might not drop to freezing but it came close. As Slocum shivered, new waves of pain rippled through his body. Any movement magnified into unbearable pain.

He watched the stars pop out. He missed the first one so he could make a wish. He was so dazed from the torture he hardly knew what to wish for. Swift death to the war party would leave him staked out to die. But if he wished to be free of his bonds, he knew how impossible it would be to fight. One of the Indians had taken his six-shooter. All of them carried rifles and knives, and two had six-shooters stuck into their waistbands.

With his trusty six-gun, he could kill many of them. Most. But he doubted his aim would be good.

What should he wish for? But it was too late. Thousands of stars blossomed in the sky, but only the first star granted a wish.

"A wish," he muttered.

"Shush."

"Wanna make a wish. Wish Marlene gets away. Thass what I wish."

A hand clamped down on his mouth to silence him.

"Are you out of your mind?"

Slocum thought he was. He saw hovering above him an oval face gently lit by the silvery moon.

"Died and gone to heaven," he said.

"I'm no good with a knife."

The sound of a blade slicing through rawhide brought him back to awareness. His right leg had been cut free. He craned his neck and looked down to see Marlene sawing away at the rawhide on his left leg.

"Hands. Get my hands free."

"When I finish here. I—"

She yelped as an Apache scooped her up and swung her about, kicking frantically. Slocum tried to pull a stake from the ground, but he couldn't. There hadn't been a guard posted so he had to believe Marlene had somehow awakened the Indian. He made no sound, probably wanting her all for himself.

She continued to fight and caused the Apache to stagger back. Slocum saw his chance and took it. He hooked his left foot in front of the warrior's foot and kicked as hard as he could with his right. His boot hit directly behind the Indian's knee, toppling him backward to land flat on Slocum's chest.

The air rushed from Slocum's lungs, but he kept kicking to tangle the brave's legs. Then he felt something hot and wet trickling down his side. The Indian grunted, rolled off Slocum onto hands and knees, and a knife blade flashed in the night.

Marlene had cut the man severely with her first thrust. The stab caught him in the back and plunged all the way through to his heart. He died instantly.

She stood upright holding the dripping knife, staring at it in horror.

"I killed him. I stabbed him in the back and killed him."

Looming behind her came the war chief.

9

"Duck!"

Slocum's warning startled Marlene, which was as good as if she had obeyed instantly. She jerked upright, stumbled over the Indian's body, and sat down heavily as the war chief swung his rifle as if it were a war club. Missing her head caused him to stagger a step.

With a powerful surge, Slocum arched his back and used all his strength locked in his legs to push himself to the left. The stake holding his right hand pulled free. He rolled and came to his knees, his left hand still fastened to the ground. Flexing his fingers did nothing to get the circulation back; the rawhide strip was still knotted around his wrist.

The chief recovered his balance, looked at Marlene, and then saw Slocum working his way to freedom. He left the woman and turned to Slocum, the rifle again whistling as it traced out a silvered arc in the moonlight. His aim was off. He missed crushing Slocum's skull. But Slocum's aim proved better. He whipped around his right arm and sent the wood stake arrowing downward into the Apache's face.

The Indian shrieked and grabbed at his injured cheek.

Slocum missed putting out the man's eye by a fraction of an inch. Pulling back, Slocum whipped the rawhide cord with its attached stake around again. This time the chief caught it with one hand and tugged. Slocum lost his balance and landed facedown. Try as he might, he couldn't yank free the stake holding his left hand. He looked up and saw the gleam in the warrior's face as he drew a knife and prepared to gut his prisoner.

Slocum got out of the way as the body fell forward, as if he died at full attention. Sticking from the man's back was the same knife used to kill the other brave.

Marlene stared at her handiwork, trembling hand over her mouth.

"I've never killed anyone," she said in a voice so low it came out as a hoarse whisper. "Tonight I killed *two*."

"Cut me free, Marlene. Marlene!" Slocum jerked hard to get the remaining stake out of the ground. His fingers felt like they would fall off at any instant. Not even a tingle in his hands hinted they were still useful for anything more than waving about.

"Marlene?" She looked at him and lowered the hand over her mouth. "I have to tell you something, Mr. Slocum."

"They're waking up in the camp. Get the knife. Cut me free!"

She fell to her knees and with both hands grabbed the hilt protruding from the war chief's back. She yanked it free then tossed it to Slocum as if it had been heated in a fire. Slocum scooped it up and dropped it. The circulation in his hands hadn't returned.

Bracing the hilt against the ground, he dragged the rawhide rope across it. Two quick swipes freed him. In spite of the need for haste with the Indians stirring in their camp, he made the effort to rub his wrists and get feeling back.

"How are we going to get away? K-Kill them all?"

Slocum would have done that if it had a ghost of a chance of succeeding. Dead men wouldn't track him to the ends of the earth because he'd killed two of their war party. He hefted the knife, considered giving it back to Marlene, then slipped it under his belt. Stretching past the woman, he grabbed the chief's fallen rifle.

He worked the lever and understood why the chief hadn't shot him when he had the chance. The magazine was empty. For all Slocum knew, the war party didn't have a cartridge among them—except the rounds in his Colt's cylinder. He dropped the useless weapon beside the chief's body.

"I fired a rifle when I was a child," Marlene said. "Let me take it. I . . . I don't want to have to stab anyone else."

"You saved my life," Slocum said. "Twice."

"You saved mine. Twice."

"It's good that we're even," he said. Taking Marlene by the arm, he pulled her away from the camp, running east down an arroyo toward low hills not far away.

The horses had been tethered on the far side of the Apache camp. Without horses, Slocum and Marlene had little chance of getting away, much less surviving the desert heat.

"Wait, the rifle!" She tried to go back and retrieve the discarded rifle.

"It's empty. All of them might be out of ammo."

"Then we—"

He clamped a hand over her mouth to silence her. Another brave had come to check his prisoner. Seconds later came the ululation to bring the rest of the war party to see that two of their number had been killed.

"The last one," whispered Marlene as they huddled close in the shelter of a boulder, "I killed. He was their leader. Won't they give up and leave us be now that he's dead?"

"Apaches elect a new war chief every time they go on the warpath. A strong leader gets elected over and over, but if one dies, another election among the band chooses a new one."

"So a new chief will want revenge?"

Slocum didn't answer. Considering the questions the dead chief had asked him, the rest of the war party wasn't likely to let him go. They thought he was a scout for the cavalry on their trail. The only way the Apaches could be sure he didn't reach the soldiers and lead them back was to kill him. And Marlene.

Now that she was with him, Slocum found his plans all jumbled up. To protect her, he had to lead the Apaches on a wild-goose chase, but they knew of her existence now. At least one of them in camp must have seen the woman. Even in the dark they had to know someone had freed Slocum because he couldn't have done it himself and killed two braves, including their chief.

He hefted the knife and wished there had been time to search the bodies for another. The rifle may have been without ammo, but any weapon trumped bare hands against angry Apaches. Silently pointing, he got the woman moving through the ravines until they came to a low rise looking back down on the Indian camp. Slocum pressed Marlene flat on the ground and flopped beside her to scout the enemy position.

"Don't stand," he said when she tried to pull away. "The moon is bright enough to cast a shadow. They can see your outline against the night sky."

"Really?" Marlene subsided, then asked, "How do you know all this?"

"I've come close to having my scalp lifted a few times."

"Oh." She started to say something more and thought better of it.

"They would have done more than lift your scalp. You'd have been lucky if they killed you outright."

"They tortured you so why wouldn't they—oh." Realization of her possible fate at the hands of the Apaches hit her. "Why wouldn't they hold me for ransom?"

"This is a war party. It's small, so they might be scouting for a larger one."

"Scouting what?"

"They wanted to know about cavalry on their trail." Slocum motioned her to silence when the Indians mounted and stowed their dead companions over horses. They rode to the east, giving Slocum the break he needed.

"Are they taking the bodies back for burial?" Marlene asked.

"Looks that way. The chief must have been more important than I thought. Otherwise, they would have buried the bodies here and kept scouting for the soldiers."

"What are we going to do, Mr. Slocum?"

"Get back to the railroad tracks and wait for the repair crew. Mad Tom has to have reached Yuma by now. It's not that far down the line." He rolled onto his side. "Sarah Jane is with the train. Your Pullman car, the tender, and locomotive were all still on the tracks."

"Back there, when you were delirious," she said, "it sounded as if you wanted to be sure Marlene was safe."

"It's my job to protect you."

"Mr. Burlison cannot be paying enough for you to risk your life so many times."

"Nope."

"Then why—oh, I understand. You're an honorable man who gave his word."

"Something like that," Slocum said. He backed down the far side of the hill before standing.

"You would have jumped into the river and done all this for Sarah Jane, too, wouldn't you?" When he didn't answer, she reached up and moved his face around so she could see his eyes. "You would have, and you aren't being paid to protect a mere maid."

Slocum refused to get into a discussion about where his duties lay.

"Even dying, your only thought was to save Marlene—me."

"I'm doing a piss-poor job of it right now unless I get you

back on the Yuma Bullet and riding fancy free to San Antonio and into your mama's arms."

"I have something to tell you that might affect how you see your duty. I—"

Slocum threw his arms around her and used his weight to knock her off her feet. Arms circling her body, they rolled downhill, Slocum taking the brunt of punishment from rocks and thorny bushes until they hit the bottom. He put his forefinger against her lips to silence her, then drew the knife and looked around. Every sense straining, he finally caught the small sounds of rocks being disturbed nearby.

Animals didn't move like that in the dark. Apaches seldom went out at night, but when they did, their need was dire.

"Stay here. If I don't come back, head straight south until you reach the tracks. Stay out of sight if you can, until the repair crew shows up."

"John, wait!"

He pulled free, shifted the knife to his left hand, and began hunting for a way to hide his approach. Keeping low, he made use of the stunted bushes the best he could, carefully avoiding the branches. Any rustling sound would alert the Apache stalking him. When he advanced another ten yards, he froze. Hunkered down, he hoped he looked like another rock at the foot of the hill.

A shadow moved within a shadow, then came out of darkness enough for him to see the Indian. Only for an instant, then the brave sank back into obscurity. Slocum gripped the knife so hard his forearm began to cramp. He forced himself to relax. It would take a few days to recover from the cuts and other tortures the Apaches had heaped on him, but he would never get the chance to soak in Marlene's fine bathtub—or one like it—if he failed now.

The Apache became restless and moved closer. Slocum waited. Patience had served him well during the war when he fought as a sniper, sitting in the crotch of a tree for hours, motionless, waiting for exactly the right shot. More than once he had turned the battle in favor of the Rebs by seeing a flash of gold braid on a Yankee officer's uniform and firing accurately. He lacked a rifle now but not the will to survive or the patience he had honed as a weapon deadlier than his marksmanship.

The Apache dropped to his knees and examined the ground. He worked toward the spot where Marlene hid, finding pebbles she had sent cascading down the hillside during her descent. As he came even with Slocum, a knife flashed in the night, rising, falling, robbing the Apache of his life before he knew he was under attack. The downward cut had entered his back to one side of his neck. From the warm pulsing flow, Slocum knew he had severed an artery but had to use his weight to pin the brave to the ground until he died. Otherwise, he would have flopped about and maybe even called out.

When the Indian lay still, Slocum rolled him over. A smile danced on his lips. He quickly unbuckled the holster around the Indian's waist and fastened it to his own. The Colt Navy came easily to hand. A quick check of the cylinder showed all the brassy rounds ready for firing. He tucked it away. To go shooting now would alert any other Indians.

In addition to the six-shooter, Slocum took another knife from the Indian's belt. He rocked back on his heels, the point aimed upward when Marlene came up.

Angrily, he said, "I could have killed you."

"There's another one behind me," she whispered.

He silently handed her the extra knife. She took it with great reluctance. He read her mind perfectly. A knife like this already had robbed two men of their lives. She had no desire to kill a third. But she would. Their lives depended on it.

"Backtrack this one's trail. I think he has a horse staked out not far off. Can you ride?"

"Of course I can," she said. "Before I was three I was on a horse." She looked embarrassed. "It wasn't much of a horse. An old Morgan too feeble for plowing, but Papa let me ride him."

"Don't spook the horse. Be sure you have the reins tight in your hands." He paused. "Wait for me if there's any question about riding the horse."

"All right," she said, pouting. "Don't treat me like a child."

"You're a child who saved my life," he said. Impetuously he kissed her and immediately regretted it. He wasn't being paid to kiss the boss's daughter. He was being paid to get her safely to San Antonio.

Hiding his lapse of good sense, he turned away from her and hurried in the direction she had come. He didn't know if it was a good thing or not that Marlene had been aware of the Indian on her trail. He approved of her alertness, but she had left a trail a blind man could follow. Then he realized this worked to their advantage. He found a hollow and lay in it, virtually invisible as the Apache sniffed out the trail, oblivious to the trap about to be sprung.

An instant before Slocum attacked, the Indian might have realized his danger. Slocum's knife flashed out, cut the brave's upper arm, and brought forth a geyser of blood and an ear-piercing scream. For a brief instant, the Apache ignored everything but the pain. Then he died, Slocum's knife driven deep into his belly.

Slocum stepped back and stared at the body. He heard a frightened horse neighing. It smelled the blood of its former rider. With measured steps, Slocum went to the horse, gentled it, and then swung onto its back. Many Indians rode with saddles now but this band did not. Whether they had raided a rancher's corral but not his tack room didn't matter to Slocum. He wasn't going to do any more walking in the burning desert.

His hand went to his six-shooter when hoofbeats approached. He relaxed when he saw Marlene astride a horse, riding bareback as easily as if she had been born there. Her knowledge continued to amaze Slocum. For a woman raised in a wealthy family, she survived out in the wilderness as well as any city dweller and better than most.

"Where now, John?"

"South to the tracks," he said. "You'll be back on your pa's railroad before you know it."

"About that," she said slowly, eyes downcast. "I've tried to tell you but something always interrupted. You see, I—"

He silenced her again.

"Hear that? Horses. Lots of them."

"The cavalry?"

"The main body of the Apaches," he said grimly. "You better clamp your thighs down because we're going to ride like the devil is after your soul."

He put his head down and showed her how to do it. If they couldn't outrun the Apaches, they were goners, and even if they reached the railroad tracks and a repair crew, they were still in danger. The crew wouldn't have the arms necessary to fight off dozens of raiders.

The night wind slipped past his face and turned warmer as dawn broke. By the time they raced across the desert less than a mile from the tracks, the Indians spotted them.

10

"There's no way we can keep going like this," Slocum said, slipping back down the sand dune and lying flat on his back to stare at the cloudless sky.

The heat built quickly, and finding water had proven to be a problem. He had misjudged where they were and had ridden a considerable distance to the south without finding the tracks. Going west would eventually bring them to the Colorado River, but Slocum had spotted another problem to wandering about aimlessly.

"How many?" Marlene asked.

Slocum appreciated how quickly she was understanding the problem.

"A couple dozen. This must be the main body of the Indians. They're going west, likely to get water from the river."

"They'd see us, wouldn't they?"

"If we tried to do the same." Growing exasperation seized him. "I took us in the wrong direction. I thought the railroad was only a few miles away."

"It might have been if we'd been closer to the river,"

Marlene said, "but it doesn't run straight east and west. Immediately after crossing the Colorado, it takes a dogleg to the southeast, angling down toward Yuma."

"How much farther do we have to ride to get to the tracks?"

Marlene shook her head. "I know there is a small station for taking on water that can't be too far away."

"Water," Slocum said. The word caused his mouth to turn even drier. "The Apaches have to know about the water tank. Why are they riding west if the station is east?" The answer worried him.

"We can find out," Marlene said. "We don't need to follow the tracks." She squinted at the sun, then drew a crude map. The wind erased her lines almost as fast as she ran her finger through the sand.

Slocum watched as she worked out where they had to ride, but he paid less attention to her drawing than to the woman. Not once had she complained. They had ridden until the horses were almost dead, then they'd dismounted and walked to rest the horses. Slocum barely had the strength to put one foot in front of another, but Marlene said nothing that didn't buoy his spirits and give him reason to keep going. How could he give up when he had to deliver her to her family in San Antonio?

"No, you wouldn't," she said, looking up.

"What's that?"

"You'll never give up. No matter what, you won't surrender, to the Indians, to the desert, to simply dying. You're a fighter, John. I hear it in your words, and I see it in the set to your shoulders. You carry yourself like a winner."

"I don't feel much like a winner," he said. Stretching caused bunched muscles to protest. His back was covered with small cuts from rocks, and his chest still leaked blood in a dozen places where the Indians had tortured him.

Marlene looked at him. He tried to decipher the message in her eyes and couldn't. She looked down in embarrassment and ran her finger in a wide circle around her map.

"I didn't mean to be so forward," she said. "It's not my place."

"Seems like whatever place that is," Slocum said, "it's where we are both stranded. How far from this sand dune to the watering station?" His finger dug down over the small X marking their destination.

"I've never had to guess such things. The times I've ridden the Yuma Bullet, I never left the train. When Mad Tom lowered the water spout, I wasn't allowed outside to watch."

Slocum found that a curious thing to say because her pa was such an important man with the railroad. Most girls in her position insisted on having their way and what employee dared deny her when a simple comment to her pa could send him on his way?

"An hour," she said suddenly. "It was an hour along the track from the bridge. That'd make the water tank thirty miles away. Or a little more because the track goes off at an angle."

"A day's ride," Slocum said. That was a hard day's ride in the desert. Without water, reaching the way station looked difficult if not impossible.

"The Indians won't be back until they've watered their horses," she said. "If we start now, we can make it after dark."

"Better to wait until it gets cooler, then ride like we mean it," Slocum said. "We can get to the station before dawn."

"I can use some rest." She rubbed her forehead and left dirty streaks. Still, sweating was a good sign.

Slocum made a crude lean-to of their blankets and let the horses rest in the dubious shade of a gangly Joshua tree. He made certain both were securely staked before dropping beside Marlene in the lean-to. Her eyelids dipped and she muttered something he couldn't understand. It sounded as if she called out her own name, but she soon drifted off to troubled sleep. He stretched out, found a comfortable position, and soon slept, only to awaken hours later. His chest boiled and salt stung the cuts. But he saw the reason for the hot band circling his body. Marlene had draped her arm over him and nestled her head into his side.

A quick look at the sun told him he had slept about five hours. It felt cooler but only because it had been such a furnace all day long. Slocum looked down at Marlene, then reached over and laid his hand on her cheek. She stirred but didn't awaken. She moved her hand up and covered his before murmuring her own name again. She came alert when he slipped his hand away.

Her green eyes went wide with panic, then she settled down.

"I had a terrible dream," she said, "but it was all right because you were there." She reached out to him, but Slocum moved back enough so she couldn't quite reach him. "Oh, I understand. It's time to go."

Seeing how she moved stirred feelings in him he tried to quash. She stretched her arms high above her head. This caused her breasts to flatten, but when she relaxed, they popped up firm and impudent. Much of her dress had been shredded again because of the fighting and riding. Before she had been shy, but now she moved in such a way as to emphasize her charms, even giving him a tantalizing glimpse of a pink nipple behind a dangling scrap of blouse.

"Will we have any trouble with the Apaches?" She brushed off sand from her skirt and turned away modestly to repair her clothing the best she could.

"I hope not." Slocum instinctively touched his six-shooter and knew a shoot-out with so many Indians ended in only one way. Even if the trusty pistol fired and all the Apaches had run out of ammo, he and Marlene would still be goners. Sheer numbers would flood over them, and the war party would show no mercy.

He watched as she swung up onto the pony. He caught a hint of bare leg all the way to the thigh, then Marlene smoothed her skirts and sat primly. With a vault he mounted his horse and got his bearings from the setting sun. Due south added to their trip, though they would reach the railroad tracks fastest that way. The way station with water had become a more enticing goal because any repair crew might find itself fighting off the Apaches.

The sun sank into the hills in the direction of the river. At first the chill felt good, then Slocum began to shiver. He saw that the desert cold caused Marlene to shudder so hard her teeth chattered. Neither said a word. They kept riding. As the stars came out, Slocum got his bearings again.

"See the bright red star? We're following it."

"Sirius?"

"Reckon I've heard it called that. A friend with a considerable amount of book learning said it's pronounced 'serious' but spelled all different. I never heard why. It's in a constellation shaped like a dog, and the dog's chasing a rabbit. I don't much see it, but folks out on night herd have to do something to keep themselves awake so they make all this up."

"Those are ancient Greek constellations," she said. Hurriedly, she added, "I read about them in a book I had once. Sirius is the brightest star in the sky, and it's in Canis Major."

"The Big Dog."

"Yes, and that's Lepus running toward Orion the Hunter."

"You've done more than read all this in a book," Slocum said.

"I spent a lot of nights outside when I was a little girl, perched in a tree, staring at the sky and wondering what's up there. You ever do that, John?"

"Wondering what's down here on the ground keeps me occupied."

They talked of nothing but comparing different diamond-hard stars as they rode until Slocum drew rein and pointed.

"See that? Starlight shining off railroad tracks."

"You see *that*?" Marlene countered. "Starlight shining off a water tank! We've found the way station!"

She started to ride, but Slocum leaned over and grabbed the reins.

"Whoa. Don't be in such a rush. Something's not right."

"It looks perfectly fine to me. There's the depot and the water tower and . . ." Her voice trailed off.

"The water spout's all broke and hanging down."

"The station master would have repaired that right away."

He bade her stay put while he dismounted and sneaked closer to the run-down building, which was hardly more than a one-room shack. A dozen yards away, an outhouse had been pushed over. Slocum saw starlight shining off the wings of bugs flying above the honey hole. Other than the loud buzz from these insects, he heard nothing.

Moving like a ghost, he pressed himself flat against the cabin wall and peered between two split planks. The interior was blacker than a coal sack. Ear against the splintery wood, he listened for any sign of life. A ragged gasping sound punctuated with tiny moans warned him of someone inside.

It also prepared him for what he found when he stepped over part of the door, which had been kicked off its hinges. The man writhing in pain on a straw pallet had to be the station master from the occasional curses he uttered.

"Did the Apaches do this to you?" Slocum asked.

The man jerked so hard he sat upright. The effort proved too much for him. He fell heavily to the pallet amid a tiny cloud of dust.

"Who're you?"

"Name's Slocum. You the station master?"

"Ned Fisk. And yeah, them Injuns ambushed me. It's dark again. They musta shot me at dawn yesterday, but I outfoxed them and hid."

Slocum had scouted the area as he worked closer to the cabin. That seemed unlikely and he said so.

Ned gasped, then laughed.

"They never thought to look in the outhouse."

"You were in the hole?"

"Naw, the outhouse. I seen 'em comin' so I pushed it over,

then crawled in. Nobody'd ever think to look in a knocked-over outhouse. They didn't."

"How'd you get so banged up?" Slocum moved closer and saw a couple bullet wounds in the man's chest.

"Cussed savages used the outhouse for target practice. I kept my tater trap shut in spite of 'em hittin' me four–five times, shootin' right through the walls. Hardest thing I ever done, not cryin' out in pain. Harder even than watchin' 'em drink my water, then break the spout so's all the rest drained out." Ned coughed again and turned to find a more comfortable position. "Gonna have the best damn crop of weeds under that water tower you ever did see. You spit on this ground here and weeds grow. You ever see a devil's claw? I got 'em all over the place. Nasty things to step on. Can ruin a horse's hoof. Goes right on through a boot, too."

Slocum knew the man rattled on to hear his own voice, to assure himself he was still alive and to bend the ear of another human being. Alone in the desert, waiting for a train to come through, had to be as lonely a job as prospecting. In its way it had to be worse. The trains stopped for only a few minutes and then left. Ned Fisk had a taste of conversation often enough, but that'd be all he ever got. A taste. A sentence or two and then the locomotive would steam on into Yuma or Deming.

Kneeling, Slocum eased open Ned's shirt and examined the wounds. He examined two in the man's chest and two more in his upper thigh. Prowling about the cabin, Slocum found a small silver flask that sloshed with liquor inside. Not much but enough for what needed to be done.

"Damn heathens took a full bottle of my firewater. Reckon they never saw a gentleman's flask so they left that. Won it in a poker game over in San Diego a couple months back, just 'fore I come out here. Fool didn't know odds and—hey, don't! Stop!"

Slocum used the brandy in the flask to cleanse the bullet

wounds. When he'd finished, hardly a drop remained, but he let Ned suck on it.

"Waste o' good peach brandy, pourin' it on my bullet holes."

Slocum probed carefully, found two slugs remained in the man's leg. The ones in his chest had gone plumb through. By the time he finished bandaging the station master up the best he could, Ned had passed out.

"Will he live?"

Slocum swung about, hand going to his six-gun. He stopped when he saw Marlene outlined in the doorway. She held a bucket.

"I told you to stay with the horse."

"I did. They're tied up under the water tower. Did the Indians destroy it?"

"You found some water?"

"The tank still has a few inches in it. I drained what I could and brought it when I heard you talking with Mr. Fisk."

Slocum said nothing. Marlene had been eavesdropping longer than she let on if she'd caught the man's name.

"He'll do just fine. He's a tough old geezer," Slocum said. He took the bucket, used the dipper to dribble water onto Ned's lips, then downed the rest himself.

"Not so fast. You'll bloat."

"Don't much care. It goes down good." He paused. "You've drunk your fill?"

"Why, no. I brought it straightaway here for him . . . and for you."

Slocum held out the dipper. Marlene came closer, then greedily drank as he tipped it over and let water drip into her mouth. Some ran down her chin and dribbled onto her bodice, causing the fabric to turn transparent and show the flesh beneath. He was sorry when the bucket ran empty.

"There's more," she said, but he wasn't sure she meant water.

Marlene reached down and pressed her hand boldly into his crotch. A little squeeze was all it took to betray his interest in her. When she felt the pulsing mound, she kept squeezing, slowly, gently, until Slocum wiggled uncomfortably at being trapped in the too-tight jeans.

"Is he asleep?" Marlene looked past Slocum at Ned Fisk.

"He's passed out, but you said there's more water in the tank?"

"And inch or two." She caught her breath when Slocum moved his hands from around her waist and up so his palms pressed down hard into her breasts.

She closed her eyes, arched her back, and shoved herself forward. He began giving those delightful mounds the same attention she gave his crotch. The tiny buttons of her nipples hardened with need and began to pulse visibly through her blouse. Slocum caught both of them between his thumbs and forefingers and slowly tweaked.

"Oh, John, John. That makes me wobbly in the knees."

She sagged against him. Her hand moved from his groin to his rock-hard belly and then slowly up across his chest until she put her arms around his neck and pulled him close for a kiss. He tasted her lips, and then her tongue began darting about until he moaned again. His hardness had reached the point where he was going to hurt himself if he didn't free himself from his jeans.

"Oh?" she said, a delightful twinkle in her emerald eyes. "Am I doing *that* to you?"

"Bitch," he said. "You know you are."

"Such language. I've never heard anyone say that about me before. What does it mean?"

"It means I'm going to take you like a dog."

"From behind?"

He spun her around, reached around her trim waist, and pressed his fingers down into her belly, then moved lower until she spread her legs. Wetness flowed from her interior as he continued to massage and stroke and move all about her privates. She shoved her ass backward into the curve of his groin.

"That's how I'm going to do it," he said. "You have any objections?"

"Yes," she said, her voice quavering with need. "You're talking and not doing!"

She hiked up her skirts and revealed her bare hindquarters. Slocum reached around and cupped one of the ass cheeks, then gave it a quick swat. Even in the dim light coming through the doorway from the starry night, he saw the red handprint forming on her sleek rump.

"More," she said, grinding her hips around and shoving back even harder. "I want more." Marlene tried to reach behind and stroke over his denim-imprisoned manhood. "You have no idea how much I want you now, John!"

He thrust forward with his hips and moved her outside into the cold night. The broken water spout dripped onto the ground, forming a mud puddle. Slocum reached down, caught up the girl, and carried her to the puddle. He let her get her feet under her, then began stripping her naked. She shimmied and held her arms over her head, helping him remove all her clothing until she stood like a marble statue in the starlight.

"Your turn," she said.

Together they got Slocum out of all his clothes until he was as naked as a jaybird, too. Then he caught her up against him and sank down to the ground, splashing about in the mud puddle.

She yelped as the cold water touched her ivory skin. Then they were rolling about in the wallow, the mud better than any feather mattress. The moisture invigorated them. Dripping water came down as they passionately struggled beneath the broken spout. Somehow they ended up with Slocum sitting cross-legged in the mud with Marlene's legs thrust out straight on either side of his hips. Facing each other, they kissed, licked, and teased lips and ears, throat and lower. She licked across his nipples, then he returned the favor.

He caught the pink buds between his lips, suckled and bit gently with his teeth, then caressed using his rough tongue until the woman shook all over. He kissed the deep valley between her breasts and finally ran his hands under her buttocks and lifted. With a smooth move, he pulled her even closer so her nether lips touched the tip of his shaft. Hands pressing on his shoulders, she eased herself down until he was buried full length within her.

They both sat for a moment, the sensations rippling through their bodies. Then neither could remain still any longer. The need was too great, the desire rampaging.

Marlene lifted and sank on his fleshy pole, twisting her hips slightly as she moved. Slocum's finger moved behind her and touched another entry to her body. She cried out when he ran his finger up her back, then her hips went berserk, flying up and down.

The water dripped down on their upturned faces, stimulating and giving excitingly different reactions as their bodies moved apart and together, grinding and thrusting.

Marlene let out a series of tiny trapped animal sounds, then howled as her body exploded in motion. She flew up and down on his length until the friction threatened to burn him to a nub. Then she quivered once and sagged against him. Slocum braced himself on the ground with his hands and continued to lift her up, driving ever deeper into her heated center until the rush of his release erupted.

Both weak and shaking from their sexual release, they clung to each other until they began to shiver in the cold.

"I never noticed how freezing it was until now," she said.

"That's because you were so hot."

"You flatter me. I . . . I've never done this before. I mean, not like this, not with . . ."

"With a hired hand?"

She giggled.

11

"He's doing much better," Marlene said, her hand pressed against Ned Fisk's cheek to check for a fever. The man stirred and a small smile came to his lips.

Slocum wondered if he played possum just to feel the woman's hand on his face. After the night they had spent together, rolling about in the mud and making love a couple times more, he had to admit the feel of her hand—and more—was worth any deception. The fact that she was the daughter of a rich and powerful railroad official hardly bothered him now, not after all they had been through together. She had saved his life and had pulled his fat from the fire. They worked together well and owed it to each other what they had done to blow off some steam.

Slocum didn't go around boasting of his conquests like so many men did, especially when they got liquored up in a saloon where they had a willing audience of sex-starved cowboys. Marlene hadn't given him any hint she was the kind to throw up an affair with a wrangler as a way of getting back at her pa for leverage in an argument either. Even if she were, Slocum thought it was worth the risk of having all the S&P Railroad bulls coming after him. What were a few more men with blood in their eyes coming after him? At least this time he had done something worthy of an army of bounty hunters calling for his hide.

He stared outside into the desert. Heaven knew he had enough angry men hunting for him. The San Diego lawmen wouldn't go beyond sight of the nearest saloon to come after him, but he doubted Big Joe Joseph gave up easily. More than the reward on Slocum's head, it was a matter of pride and he had been humiliated in full sight of a crowd. He had a reputation to uphold, and bringing Slocum in—dead—was the best way Big Joe had of doing that.

The only way, Slocum thought, that the bounty hunter could find him was if someone at the S&P rail yard mentioned how Morgan Burlison had hired a new bodyguard for his daughter. Catching the Yuma Bullet had been a boon for Slocum, taking him away from a world of bullets and gunsmoke.

A wry smile curled his lips as he looked back over his shoulder at Marlene putting a damp cloth on Fisk's forehead. Shooting it out with Big Joe held no appeal, and he had been through hell since crossing the Colorado River, but he had fought Indians before, endured hardships that were worse— and with less reward. Marlene was worth walking through hell barefoot for. The smile died when he knew it had to come to an end soon enough.

The repair crew would come steaming out of Yuma and get them back on the tracks toward San Antonio. Parting with Marlene would be a heartbreaker, but Slocum faced it as something needful. Their worlds couldn't be any different. She lived amid wealth and power. More often than not, Slocum had no idea where his next meal was coming from, and a shot of whiskey gave the only release from the aches and pains of a long day in the saddle.

"What's that?" Slocum asked. He left the doorway and felt the warmth rolling in as the sun rose to heat the desert again.

Marlene looked up. Her eyes were wide and bright and he wanted to kiss her, but over in the corner of the cabin lay something he had missed before. He went to it and began pulling away the debris tossed on it by the Indians as they ransacked the cabin.

"A telegram key!" Marlene came to him and rested her hand on his shoulder as he dug through the pile of splintered wood and ripped cloth. "And the batteries! We can send a message!"

"The wires aren't attached," Slocum said. He cleaned off a spot on the floor and hauled over the heavy batteries. The Indians had missed them entirely, or they knew how dangerous they were if the contents spilled. The sulfuric acid chewed through flesh and cloth in nothing flat. "There, all hooked up."

Marlene gripped his shoulder even tighter and her breath came faster in anticipation of more immediate rescue.

"Can you send a message?"

"I know a little Morse code," Slocum said. "Most of the traffic on the telegraph is special code swapped between two operators and doesn't mean squat."

"I always wondered. They want it to seem more difficult than it is so they can charge such outrageous prices. Why, once I paid almost three dollars for a telegram and—" Marlene cut off her reminiscence when Slocum looked up at her.

"Three dollars? For someone like you, that's a drop in the bucket."

"Sorry. Can you send a telegram?"

Slocum turned to the chore. He wiped his hands on his jeans, then touched the key. A real telegrapher called it a bug. Slocum would crush it if it failed to work. He tapped it a couple times and was rewarded with a small spark and a loud click. Chewing his tongue in concentration, he composed and sent a short message, then sat back.

"That ought to do it. Not sure where I sent it, but the wires go both ways."

"So it alerted them in both San Diego and Yuma?"

Slocum grunted assent. His spelling wasn't the best at any time, but just sending out the message alerted any telegrapher to the problem at the watering depot. However, something worried him.

"Wire won't go to San Diego. Lost it a week back where it goes over the Colorado bridge," came Ned's cracked voice.

"But to Yuma?" Slocum asked.

"You didn't get a click back."

"What's that?" Marlene asked.

"Acknowledgment the message got through. You aren't such a bad telegrapher," Ned said to Slocum. "Slow but you got the knack."

"What would the acknowledgment sound like? There hasn't been any message come in since I hooked up the wires."

"None? Yuma's a busy station. There shoulda been something," Ned said. He sank down to the pallet, closed his eyes, then finally said, "Damned Injuns must have cut the wire 'tween here and Yuma."

"But he sent the message!"

"It's like talking without anyone to listen," Slocum said. "The Apaches cut the line before they attacked, to be sure no warning was sent about their whereabouts."

"Then we just have to wait," Marlene said. Her dejection showed in her slumping shoulders and downcast expression.

"I can find the cut wire and fix it," Slocum said. "Where's your spare telegraph wire and cutters?"

Ned perked up.

"You know how them varmints work? They tie rawhide onto a wire 'fore they cut the line."

"Why would they do that?" Marlene asked, frowning.

"So it's harder to find," Slocum explained. "A wire on the ground is obvious. One whose color hardly changes from insulation to rawhide takes up time to find. A nearsighted rider might pass right on by and never know where the trouble is."

"You said it, mister. You ever a telegrapher?"

Slocum had worked at about every job possible but had only a passing knowledge of what it took to be a telegraph operator. He followed Ned's quick glance to a crate on the other side of the cabin and took out wire and cutters.

"How much of that wire you figuring on using?" Ned asked.

"As much as it takes. I'll return what I don't use." Slocum suspected the railroad made Fisk buy his own tools and wire. "If they only cut a foot or so, I'll bring back most of it."

"Naw, don't go doing that. Find the cut, splice in on one side, and let the extra wire droop on down to the ground. Keeping the wire taut between poles is a skill not many folks have."

Slocum hefted the wire and tool and went outside. Marlene followed.

"You be careful. This isn't dangerous, is it? Climbing up a pole and fixing the break?"

"I'll be back before you know it. The Apaches wouldn't have cut the wire more than a mile or two away from this station. If they'd cut it sooner, Yuma would notice. More than that, Ned would have noticed his key going down, and giving too much warning makes it more likely they'd get shot at."

"You listen to me, John Slocum. Be very careful." She stood on tiptoe and gave him a quick kiss. Then she threw her arms around his neck and pulled him down for a more satisfying kiss. Panting for breath, flushed, and looking a bit wild and scared, she backed off. She covered her well-kissed lips with a hand and averted her gaze, again the shy young girl.

"With a sendoff like that, what's the return celebration going to be like?"

She jerked up to face him, startled. Then she got a sly look and said, "You'll have to return to find out!"

Happy to see her less fearful, Slocum jumped onto his captured horse and rode away. He pulled down the brim of his Stetson to shield his eyes from the sun and watch the smooth flow of the black-wrapped telegraph wire. Jockeying around, he caught the right angle to reflect a bright silver dot off the wire. If it changed, he would have found his break.

A half hour later the bright dot disappeared, then returned a few feet farther along the wire. Slocum drew rein, squinted, and worked around to the other side of the wire. Sure enough, a couple feet of rawhide had been spliced into the wire. No signal went beyond this point.

Slocum looked around and saw a small stand of cottonwoods. He tethered his horse in their shade and hiked back to the telegraph pole nearest the break. Studying the matter, Slocum decided it would be easy enough to do as Ned had suggested. Splice a long piece of wire to the stub near the pole, then let the longer section drop to the ground, but wasting wire to run from the stub to the fallen end rankled. He could repair the line without letting fifty feet of wire flop down onto the ground.

He cut off a long loop of the wire and whipped it around the telegraph pole before twisting the ends tight behind him. The wire let him lean back and jam his feet down into the wooden pole to climb more easily. As a kid in Georgia, he was second best only to his brother, Robert, at skinning up a tree and finding the highest point to stare across the fields in their boyish competitions. Slocum worked his way up to the crosspiece holding a glass insulator. The telegraph wire ran around it and continued on to the way station. Bending close to the pole and reaching around, he felt the hard knot in the rawhide where the Indians had cut the wire and tied the strip that smothered any signal.

Working carefully, not wanting to start over, he spliced in the length of wire he held between his teeth, then played it out to cut the rawhide and securely splice the other end. As he finished, hoofbeats caused him to crane his neck. An

Apache brave rode slowly along the railroad tracks, eyes downcast. Slocum tucked the wire cutters into his gun belt, then slipped his Colt out, and took aim.

He wanted a good shot. Waiting until he was getting antsy proved how keyed up he was. Slocum's patience usually knew no bounds. As the brave came under him, Slocum squeezed the trigger. The hammer felt on a punk round with a dull *click!*

The Indian looked around at the noise. When he failed to find the source of the deadly sound, he glanced up and saw Slocum. The Indian grabbed for a bow slung in front of him. Slocum watched the smooth movements as the brave whipped out an arrow, nocked it, and raised the weapon to send a shot upward to skewer Slocum.

The Indian was fast. Slocum was faster. He cut the wire around his waist and fell straight down, atop the warrior. He used the butt of his six-shooter to hammer at the brave's head. A glancing blow knocked the Indian from his horse. Slocum got his feet under him to face the angry warrior.

A knife gleamed in the sunlight as the Indian advanced. Slocum lifted his Colt Navy and fired again. This time the bullet sang out and flew straight to the enemy's heart. The Indian took two more steps before realizing he had been shot dead. Collapsing at his enemy's feet, the Apache gave one last twitch and died. Slocum stepped back and holstered his pistol. It had come through for him when it mattered most.

Dragging the Indian to the stand of cottonwoods, he propped the dead man up before fetching his horse. Two horses ensured his safe return. He could ride one until it tired, then jump onto the other and finish the ride at top speed. He took the time to dig a decent grave. He wanted to avoid a pack of coyotes coming to feast. Another Indian might notice and investigate. The longer before this brave was discovered, the better it was for him, Marlene, and Ned Fisk.

Slocum looked up the pole at his handiwork. The splicing held. He galloped back along the tracks and switched mounts just a quarter mile away from the depot. He saw Marlene standing in the shade waiting for him. Waving, she stepped out and gave him the best reason in the world for returning. Her smile was nothing but sincere at seeing him again.

"Where'd you get the other horse?" she asked. "It's another Indian pony. Were you attacked?"

"I did the attacking after I mended the line. Has anything come in?"

"Ned has been hunkered down by it for the past hour."

"That's about when I repaired it." Slocum jumped to the ground and secured the reins of both horses to a rusted section of railroad track discarded beside the station house.

As anxious as he was to hear what Ned had received— and sent—he still took the time to properly kiss Marlene. She clung to him and sobbed just a little.

"What's wrong? You're crying."

"I worried I wouldn't see you again. Then the telegraph began clacking, and you didn't come back."

"I can't travel as fast as the signal along the wire. That's why we use telegraphs."

"I know," she said, squeezing him hard. "I know it but I didn't *know* it, if you can understand."

They went inside. Slocum saw Ned hunched over the key, fingers flying as the code left along the repaired wire.

"Glad you're back. Got the telegraph working."

"Have you sent a message to Yuma yet?" Slocum asked.

"I did. Bad news. The Yuma Bullet isn't able to start back right away. The Apaches pulled up track between here and there. Worse, they pulled out the spikes holding the track in place. If a locomotive rolls over a section without spikes, it'll derail."

"They're fixing the track, aren't they?"

"Yes, sir, they are, but they got to go slow. On foot and check every rail, every spike, to be certain."

"How far away are they working? They can back the Yuma Bullet up to that point and we can join them there."

"Might be an idea." Ned worked on the key and finally deciphered the return code. "More 'n ten miles away. Might be closer to fifteen."

"We can all go, John. You have a third horse now."

Ned looked curious at where the horse had come from but shook his head.

"I'm not leaving my post. Don't feel like enduring the desert just to have some doctor say I'm fine and then the company sends me back and I'm better off staying here in the first place and—"

"I get the idea," Slocum said. He took Marlene aside and spoke in a low voice. "He's going to be all right. Do you want to ride to the crew? They'll have the tracks inspected in another couple days."

"There might be more Apaches out there," she said. Her face screwed up in thought. Then she said, "Let's go right away. Ten or fifteen miles is only a half-day's ride."

"Let's get what water we can and get on the trail," Slocum said.

He didn't want to return Marlene to her people this fast, but that was selfishness on his part. Ned had sent the message that she was unharmed. Morgan Burlison might want to have her in the hands of his railroad employees without delay.

The two of them rode from the way station, not speaking but occasionally glancing at each other knowing this was going to be the last time they had together. Slocum wanted to ask her to ride north with him and to hell with San Antonio and her family, but he knew this was selfishness on his part. And he had his duty. He had been hired to see her safely home. No matter what he felt for her, that had to be his first concern.

It still hurt like hell.

12

"John, there's someone lying in the dirt. Up ahead, by the tracks. Do you see him?"

Slocum snapped alert. He had been riding along, dozing. The heat wore him down and stole away his senses. Every drop of sweat on his body found a spot to sting, making him wonder if he had any inch of skin left intact. A quick swipe of his bandanna took the sweat off his forehead and let him focus on the ground. Silver shimmers masked the tracks, the heat rising from the cinders used as ballast to hold the rails in place. To touch the black cinders or the steel rails meant a serious burn.

"It's a man, and he's moving. He's waving to us!"

"Stay here," Slocum said. "The Apaches might be using him as bait."

"Don't be ridiculous. I don't see anything else alive out there. The land is as flat as an ironing board." Marlene sniffed. "And twice as hot, I daresay. Where would Indians hide?"

Slocum wasn't inclined to argue with her, but the Apaches could disappear into desert like this better than a lizard. A small rise could conceal a half-dozen braves, and the mirages caused by heat boiling up off the tracks hid all details close to the ground. An Apache or two could lie there and never be seen until a rider came on top of them. He slipped the leather thong off his six-shooter's hammer and trotted forward, ahead of the woman. If any shooting started, he wanted to be a shield between her and the worst of it.

The nearer he got to the man, the less likely an ambush seemed. The ragged man tried to stand, then fell back when his legs refused to hold him. Slocum had seen good actors in his day. No one faked weakness this well.

"I'll give him some water." Marlene rode past and slipped to the ground, carrying a canteen they had taken from Ned Fisk.

"Ma'am, please, dyin' here. Need water. Need it bad!"

She sloshed some on his dust-caked, dried lips. The man greedily grabbed for the canteen but Marlene agilely avoided him.

"Not too much too soon. You'll cramp up if you do." She gave him a little more. When she finally allowed him a bigger drink, she had to fight to pull it from his grasp.

"You're strong enough," Slocum said, looking down on the man. He had ridden around so he and his horse cast shadows over the man. Being out of the burning sun revived him as much as the water. "How'd you get out here all by your lonesome?"

"You're not one of the railroad repair crew," Marlene said. "They have a distinctive . . . odor." She sniffed and recoiled. Even from his perch atop the horse, Slocum caught the same odor. It was bad enough to gag a maggot.

"Nope, me and my family, we was headin' on north."

"Through the desert in the middle of the day?" Slocum wondered about that.

"We bought a map down south. The feller what sold it to us said this was safe, easy. We paid him ten silver pesos for it."

"How did you end up in the desert all alone?" Marlene asked, concerned.

"Reckon that was all my fault. I was settin' in the back of the wagon and dozed off. Musta fell off and nobody noticed." The man rubbed the back of his head, where a knot the size of a hen's egg poked through his thinning hair. He had sunburned on his bald pate and the back of his neck.

Slocum knew he would have been a goner in another hour if they hadn't come along. But he looked down the tracks and felt uneasy about everything. The locomotive or the repair crew ought to have been in sight by now. The man added a new problem he wasn't too keen on solving, but Marlene obviously had other ideas.

"We can give him the spare horse, John. He can catch up with his family."

"Ma'am, I appreciate that. Don't know how to thank you." He took a step forward and collapsed.

Marlene knelt at his side in an instant. She looked up, and Slocum knew what she was going to say before the words burned his ears.

"We can catch up to the wagons and get him back to his people. It won't take long, John. We have to!"

"Better to keep him with us and find the repair crew."

"He might never be with his family again! And you know that map is bogus. So do I. We can tell them they've been rooked."

"I owe it to your pa to get you back safely and not go running off on wild-goose chases."

"They can't be more than an hour ahead. He would have died in that time."

Slocum saw a dust cloud not a mile to the north and gave in to the inevitable.

"It might be dangerous. You stay and I'll—"

"You'll need my help. Why, you can't just drape him over the horse and ride with him like that."

Slocum had intended doing that very thing.

The man moaned and settled the matter. Slocum dismounted, heaved the man over his horse, then rode behind him, arms circling the man's body to hold him upright. The horse protested against the double weight, but Marlene assured him they would switch to the spare pony when the burdened one began flagging.

Slocum fumed. It wasn't his job to take care of anyone but Marlene. The way she insisted on this act of charity made it impossible to deny her, though. Slocum slowly began to wonder if he had the wrong idea about rich girls and their fathers. Morgan Burlison seemed anxious about his daughter's safety, and Marlene certainly cared for others— including a stranger she'd found half dead in the desert. Slocum couldn't get it out of his head how she had asked after Sarah June when her own life had hung in the balance as she was almost swept away in the Colorado River.

"John, ahead! Do you see it?"

He glumly nodded. The dust kicked up by wheels obscured the wagon and team pulling it along. He shifted, touched his Colt, and got a groan from the man propped up in front of him on the saddle.

"You spot 'em? They in sight?"

"Get down. You can walk the rest of the way."

"It . . . it's not far, is it?" The man landed on his feet and walked along, stronger than he had appeared while weighing down Slocum's horse.

Slocum rested his hand on his Colt but did not draw. Something didn't set right with him.

"They're sure as hell gonna be surprised to see me come walkin' up like this. Them fools think I'm still settin' on the back of the last wagon."

"I doubt that," Slocum said. "The trailing wagon's not got its rear gate down. You weren't sitting there."

"They done switched positions in the line then," the man said. "The one wagon that's in front now. Thass the one where I was."

Marlene listened to the byplay. She swung in the saddle to ask the question that had already been answered in Slocum's head. He was drawing his six-shooter when the man reached up, grabbed his gun arm, and yanked hard, unseating Slocum. When he hit the ground, the six-gun discharged, but the man swarmed over Slocum, pummeling him with bony fists. One connected, but not before Slocum got off a second shot, better aimed than the first. The man grunted but kept coming after him until another punch landed on the side of Slocum's head, knocking him senseless.

He gripped hard on his six-shooter, but the man pried it loose and stumbled away, clutching the captured iron in both hands. Dazed, Slocum shook his head to clear his vision. When he did, he faced the scrawny man, who held the six-shooter in steady hands. The pistol's small bore might as well have been a .45 from the way it looked to Slocum. All he saw was death pointed at him.

"Gotcha now, you son of a bitch. You ain't gittin' the better of Cantankerous Jim." The man steadied the pistol, then cocked it, and squeezed the trigger.

For a heart-stopping instant, Slocum thought he was a goner. But the hammer fell on another punk round. A tiny *pop!* sounded as the slug made its way from the barrel but got no farther. With a spring like a cougar, Slocum launched himself and came up under Jim's arms. Still woozy from the blow to his head, Slocum failed to knock over his foe.

Jim hit him on the back with the pistol butt, but in doing so he lost his footing. They went down in a thrashing pile, neither doing a good enough job of damaging the other to end the fight. Several heavy strikes from the pistol butt landed on Slocum's shoulder, sending sharp pain rocketing through his body. Rather than slowing him, this burned away the fog in his head and made him a fiercer fighter.

His arms circled Jim's body but failed to gain an advantage. Slocum's feet slipped and slid on the dry, sunbaked earth. In the distance he heard Marlene screaming and then her cries suddenly choked off.

"Stop that there fightin' or I slit the filly's throat."

Slocum took advantage of Jim's surprise at hearing the threat. He knocked him to his back, scrambled around, and pulled the man upright to use the scrawny man as a shield. With his arm circling Jim's throat, Slocum got a better look at the problem.

A man who might have been Jim's pa held a knife to Marlene's throat. The threat of a quick slash was all too real.

Slocum tried to gain the advantage.

"I'll break his neck if you don't let her go." He tightened his grip and forced a gasp of pain from Jim.

"Now, boy, that ain't no kinda threat. I was the one what slugged the son of a bitch and throwed him off the wagon."

"Pa, don't let him kill me!"

"Why the hell not? She's purtier than you, and you was stealin' from me. You was stealin' from your whole damn family!"

"I kin explain!"

"John!" Marlene jerked as the blade pressed into the side of her throat.

"What we have here is a Mexican standoff," Slocum said.

"Don't see it that way a'tall. I got nuthin' to lose if you kill that piece o' shit son o' mine. You got this purty girl's life to lose. And then what you gonna do? You cain't fight the lot of us."

For the first time Slocum tore his gaze from the knife at Marlene's throat to the other three men watching. They laughed and swapped money, betting on the outcome. If everyone died, they would get as much enjoyment from it as a weekend drunk in a whorehouse.

"Let her go, I'll let this one go, and we'll be on our way."

"Now that don't look like a good deal to me. I gotta give up this bitch, and I don't wanna do that, no siree." The man's eyes flickered toward the horses.

"I'll throw in a horse. You can use another horse," Slocum said, realizing he had to resolve this fast. The longer it went on, the less likely Marlene was to escape with nothing more than a shallow cut on her neck. The men he faced were as crazy as bedbugs.

"One horse? Thass all? Two!"

"Release her and I'll give you two. Your choice."

"Them's Injun ponies."

"I took them from an Apache war party."

"Thass right brave of you, sneakin' up in the middle of the night and rustlin' their horses."

"I killed their riders," Slocum said harshly. He gave Jim's neck a crank and got a frightened cry he hoped would deter the others from doing anything too extreme with the knife held to Marlene's throat.

"Deal," Jim's pa said. "You gather up them reins and walk the horses over to the back wagon, tether 'em, and me and you'll release our prisoners at the same time."

Slocum dragged Jim around, forced him down onto his knees, and then plucked up the Colt. It might have misfired but it had fired a couple rounds before. One of the remaining cartridges might serve him. After all, his luck had to change sooner or later.

"Get the reins," Slocum said, manhandling Jim. With all three horses being led forward, it became harder to hold on to the man.

They reached the trailing wagon.

"Go on 'n' tie up them horses." Jim's pa loosened his hold on Marlene and took the knife from her throat.

Jim fumbled and dropped the reins. Slocum kept Jim between him and the other men. "Pick up the reins," he ordered.

"John! Look out!"

From the corner of his eye, Slocum saw movement. Images blurred together. A hand. A black frying pan. A faded gingham dress. Then the iron skillet struck him smack on the top of the head with enough force to drive him to the ground. He tried to hang on to the six-shooter, to fire it, to get one round into Jim's good-for-nothing gut, but he had been too battered and beaten to keep his grip.

A second blow knocked him flat. He felt Jim snatching the gun from his grip again. This time came a woman's voice to go along with the humiliation.

"I beaned the son of a bitch right proper, didn't I, Pa?"

"You surely did, Ma. And now we got ourselves a brand-new member of the family. Say howdy to your new ma, girl."

Slocum heard Marlene's cry of pain before he blacked out.

13

Warmth covered him like a fuzzy cotton blanket. He wanted nothing more than to curl up next to the fire and sleep for another few hours before he had to get up and chop wood for the day. Slocum rolled onto his side and tried to pull up the blanket. Somewhere in the back of his mind he realized there wasn't any blanket and he didn't have to get up to chop wood or do any other chore.

All he had to do was die.

He sputtered and spat dirt from his mouth. He tried to open his eyes, but the intense sunlight shining on his face caused him to squeeze his eyes tightly shut. He curled up into a tighter ball and felt the brittle ground underneath crackle and break like glass. Worse, the sharp edges of dried earth cut into him. Force of will allowed him to roll onto his belly, then come to hands and knees. This simple move took all his strength. He stayed this way, head hanging down and out of the direct sunlight for an eternity, but when he forced his eyes open again, he saw what he feared.

The family had abandoned him in the desert just as they had Cantankerous Jim. He rocked back and realized his

Stetson was gone. The once fancy clothing he had taken from Morgan Burlison hung in tatters. Burning sun pouring through the rips seared his skin. He got to his knees, then stumbled to his feet. No hat mattered more to him than anything else. With hands more like blunt clubs, he pulled up the coat and fastened it in place over his head using his bandanna. Relief came almost as painfully as the sunlight.

Cantankerous Jim or his pa had taken his six-shooter and hat. If his clothing had been anywhere near its former magnificence, they would have taken that. Only being as disheveled as Jim and his family had saved Slocum from being stripped naked and left in the desert. For whatever reason, they had left him with his boots.

He had his life, his battered boots, and a growing cold fury that could only be extinguished by death, whether it was his own or theirs. Slocum took a step and then another and another until he built up enough momentum to keep going without thinking about how hard it was simply to walk. When he crossed the wagon tracks, he turned and went north. The three wagons had been moving that way. He saw no reason for them to reverse course simply because they had left him for dead and taken Marlene hostage.

Marlene. Marlene. For a few steps the name bounced around in his skull but produced no picture. Who was she? Then he remembered. His step became firmer. He had a job to do. He had revenge to exact from the hides of a scavenger family.

"If you've touched her, you'll pray for me to cut your throats. If you've touched her, you'll die out here like you wanted me to do—after I get done teaching you a lesson."

He saw how the wagon tracks went around a sunbaked hill. Slocum kept moving, going to the top of the sand dune to get a better idea where the travelers had gone. Using his hand to shield his eyes, he blinked when he saw the wagons not a hundred yards off. He couldn't believe he had been in the sun long, but the wagons should have gotten farther, even in a few minutes.

Then he saw Jim and his pa with another of the sons standing by a wagon canted to one side. Slocum's water-deprived brain finally pieced everything together. One wagon had lost a wheel or maybe an axle had broken. Whatever caused the short caravan to halt gave Slocum his chance. Tracking them over miles would have meant his end.

He sat heavily when Jim turned and looked in his direction. Slocum remained motionless as Jim scanned the side of the dune, then turned his attention back to the damaged wagon when his pa shoved him. This caused a minor scuffle that involved all the men. Slocum scooted down the side of the dune, knowing they would never notice him in the heat. As filthy as he was, he looked like part of the hillside.

A quick search of his clothes revealed no weapon. He knew they had stolen his Colt Navy. They had also taken his knife. Reaching out, he found a sharp-edged rock small enough to rest in the palm of his hand. Using his bandanna, he wrapped it up and swung it a few times. It had heft, the stony edges were like razors, and using it like a flail added to the destruction it could cause if he landed it on one of their heads.

The sun dipped lower and cast shadows across the desert. As anxious as Slocum was to take on the family, he waited until the air turned cold. For a few minutes it invigorated him. Then the bone-chilling cold worried away as much of his strength as the hot sun had. He got to his feet, walked around until he felt stronger, then lit out for the wagons.

A small cooking fire brought the odors of boiling coffee and a mess of cooking beans to torment him. His mouth tried to water and couldn't. His belly grumbled so loudly that he worried they would hear him coming.

The argument going on between the family hid any sound he might have made as he crept closer. He almost abandoned his attempts at stealth when he saw Marlene. They had tied her spread-eagle to a wagon wheel. She had been stripped to the waist, her legs sticking out bare from under her bunched skirts around her waist. Her head lolled. For all he knew, she had died.

This fed the need for revenge. Four men—three sons and the pa—sat around the fire arguing while the old woman dished out the beans and poured the coffee. She never shut up, a constant barrage of complaints and insults issuing from her razor-slash of a mouth until her husband cuffed her, then bitched about her spilling his coffee when she stumbled.

"I gotta take a leak," one brother said, getting to his feet.

"What, you want me to hold it fer you? Don't piss too close to camp like you done before."

"Aw, Pa, t'warn't my fault it stunk to high heaven. How was I to know that was skunk cabbage I et?"

Slocum stopped beside the disabled wagon. A quick look showed the nut had cracked, causing the wagon wheel to fall off. Fixing it was the work of a few minutes, but with these shirkers they'd likely abandon the wagon rather than work to fix it.

The man looking to empty his bladder passed within a few feet of Slocum but never noticed the unwanted intruder to his camp. He was too intent on finding a greasewood bush to water. He found one not five feet away and worked to unbutton his fly. Slocum swung his weapon around a few times to get the feel of it. The sound of the sling swishing alerted the man.

"That you, Jim? Yer bladder's as weak as mine."

He half turned, expecting to see Cantankerous Jim. Instead he saw death wrapped in a bandanna swing up and descend. He tried to fend it off with both hands and sprayed piss all around. The dull *thunk!* as Slocum drove the rock into the top of the man's head was followed by a gasp before the man died.

Off balance, Slocum tripped over the body. He dropped down, his knee driving into the dead man's chest just to be sure he would stay down. Panting from the exertion, Slocum bent over, caught his breath, and then recovered enough to search the corpse.

A knife gleamed in the starlight as Slocum slid it from a sheath and held it high. Strength flowed back with the weapon in his hand.

He whirled about and stalked toward the dark wagons. The firelight flickered and caused shadows to dance as the men moved around the fire, shoving each other and making rude comments while the woman cleaned up after the sparse supper. Slocum dropped to his belly, crawled under the wagon, and came up behind the wheel where Marlene was bound.

"You still alive?" His whisper came out raspy, and when he got no reply, he wondered if he had even spoken. Before he could speak louder, the woman moved, straining against the ropes holding her wrists. "Don't move. I'll get rid of them and we can get out of here."

"Free me. Please. I can't stand being like this one second longer."

"Grab hold of the wheel so it won't look like I cut your ropes." He waited until her fingers curled around the smooth spokes before using the knife to saw through the tough hemp bonds.

"Faster. I want to get circulation back into my hands."

"The knife's dull."

"So are they. They . . . they're animals."

Slocum didn't ask what they had done to her. This wasn't the time or place, and he wasn't sure he wanted to know.

At last the blade dragged across the ropes enough times to sever them. Marlene sagged forward, but she held on grimly and even pulled herself up straighter to make it appear the ropes still held her.

"Kill them, John. Kill them all."

Her tone cut through his soul. Marlene spoke with no passion at all. No hatred, no burning desire to see Jim and his kin dead. That neutral tone told him something had died within her because of this nasty family.

He scooted back and got to his feet behind the wagon.

"Zeke, where you at?" Jim came around the wagon. "You pissin' yer brains out again? I tole you what it was like gettin' the clap, but you didn't listen."

Slocum judged his distance and struck, the knife swinging in an arc that ended in the man's gut. The impact echoed all the way up his arm to his shoulder, causing him to step back a pace. Jim grabbed his belly and bent over. He looked up, eyes wide with fear. A hand came from his stomach black with his blood.

"You! You done stabbed me!"

Slocum saw what had happened. Jim wore Slocum's cross-draw holster and the knife point had cut deep into the leather and failed to penetrate more than an inch.

"Pa! He's back. Pa!"

That cry was the last sound to come from Cantankerous Jim's mouth. Slocum's second cut drew the blade across his throat. Dull, the blade tore rather than cut all the way to his spine. Jim fell away and crashed to the ground, flailing about dead and not knowing it yet.

Slocum dived down and ripped at the gun belt, unbuckling it and slinging it around his own middle. The weight of his Colt Navy on his left hip gave him new confidence that he could take the entire family. He pulled it and looked up to see the third brother raring back with an axe in his hands.

The six-shooter fired. The sound told Slocum the round wasn't at full strength, but it sent the bullet tearing up and into the man's chin. The top of his head exploded and sent a rain of blood backward.

"I'll kill the son of a bitch!" The woman shrieked and ran at Slocum with the frying pan he remembered too well from his earlier encounter.

He aimed and pulled the trigger. The six-shooter had given him all it could. He twisted to the side and avoided having his head bashed in again by the fiercely cursing woman. Swinging his boot back, he caught her behind the knee and sent her to the ground.

Spitting like a cat, she kept swinging the frying pan. Bits of hot grease from it spattered Slocum in the face. Each drop burned like fire as it clung to his cheeks. He scrambled to get away. She didn't retreat. Instead, she got to her feet and came after him, fingers curled into talons. The look on her weathered, haggard face wasn't human. As she hissed and spat, she clawed for his eyes.

Slocum turned half away, then unleashed a haymaker that connected with her cheek. Her head snapped back, her eyes rolled up in her head, and she fell rigidly to the ground.

"You kilt her! You done kilt her and my boys! You're a dead man. You shoulda died in the desert, but now I'll make sure you breath yer last."

Jim's pa raised a shotgun and sighted along the double barrels in Slocum's direction. With nowhere to dodge, Slocum waited to die.

"Oh," Jim's pa said. His finger came back on the double triggers. One barrel discharged into the ground and the other failed to fire.

He fell forward, momentarily impaling himself on his shotgun. He hung balanced, his chest pressing into the stock with the muzzle crammed into the ground. Then he slid to the side and lay still. Slocum rushed forward, kicked the shotgun away, and saw there wasn't any need for that. A knife had been sunk to the hilt in the man's back.

Slocum looked up at Marlene. She was a wild and barbaric figure, naked to the waist, her torn skirts flopping about her legs. She breathed hard as she stared at the man she had killed.

"He left his knife by the fire," she said. "I killed him with his own knife." She used both hands to brush through her tangled hair, straightened, and looked hard at Slocum. "I'm glad I killed him. He deserved it." She looked past him to the woman. "But not as much as her. You kill her?"

Slocum checked. His powerful blow had broken her neck. He nodded.

"Too bad. I wanted to kill her with my bare hands for what she did to me."

"Her? Not the men?"

"Her," Marlene said. She tried to spit but her mouth was drier than the desert.

Slocum went to her, not sure what to do. Then she came into his arms. They clung to each other without speaking. Marlene didn't sob or quake. She had been pushed past such emotions. After an eternity, she thrust back to put a bit of space between them and looked up at him.

"What now?"

"We've got plenty of supplies. We take what we need and ride like kings," he said.

"To the tracks?"

He wondered at her tone. She sounded as if she wanted him to say they were continuing north and abandoning the Yuma Bullet and reaching San Antonio and everything else Morgan Burlison had hired him to do.

"Help me sort through everything," he said. He had to keep her busy, her mind off what had happened. "We'll drive out right away. Tonight."

Marlene silently tossed what few usable items she found into one wagon, then sat in the driver's box, hands folded in her lap. She had pulled her blouse about her shoulders but was still more naked than clothed. When Slocum offered her one of the old woman's shawls, she shoved it away and threw it onto the arid ground without making a sound other than a single animal-like growl.

In less than a half hour, Slocum had the team hitched, their three horses tied to the back of the wagon, and started south to find the railroad tracks and a way to return to civilization.

Marlene didn't say a word until sunup when they spotted the tracks. What she said then startled him.

14

"Don't take me back. Please, John. Don't."

Slocum looked at the woman. Her face was drawn and dirty. Tears had left streaks as they trickled down her cheeks. He had sensed reluctance before but decided that what the scavenger family had done had affected her so much she wasn't thinking straight. Now that Marlene had had an entire night to reflect on her captivity, she still wanted to turn tail and run.

"Your family won't think poorly of you because of what happened," Slocum said. "They don't ever have to know. I won't say a word."

"What? My family? Oh, them. No, it's not that way, John. I've wanted to tell you something ever since you saved me from drowning. Back at the river. You see, I—"

Slocum shot to his feet and shielded his eyes.

"Damnation, I don't believe it."

"You knew? That I—"

"He's still on my trail," Slocum said. "He's a force of nature." His hand touched the butt of his useless six-shooter. He twisted around and dived headfirst into the wagon bed, throwing what they had salvaged around until he found the double-barreled shotgun.

"John, what's going on?"

"The rider. He's on my trail. I can't let him catch me."

"What rider?" Marlene stood and stared in the direction of the railroad tracks. "I see him. A big man, wearing a fringed jacket. Who is he?"

"A bounty hunter intent on taking me in for a reward."

"You're a wanted man?"

"The marshal in San Dismas got it all wrong. That's not going to stop that bounty hunter out there from taking me in."

"If you're innocent, explain it."

"Big Joe Joseph doesn't intend for me to explain. He'll take me in dead because if I can convince the marshal I'm innocent, there isn't a five-hundred-dollar reward to collect."

"That's terrible. You can't be expected to clear your name if he kills you."

Slocum found a box of shells, ripped it open, and took two out. They slid easily into the shotgun's chambers. A quick snap closed the breech.

"I'll tell him you didn't do whatever it is the marshal accused you of. He'll listen."

Slocum pulled up the canvas and pressed his eye to the small opening. The bounty hunter rode toward them. A dozen things ran through Slocum's mind. He wasn't up for a drawn-out fight, but murdering Joseph in front of Marlene didn't sit well with him either. What she thought of him mattered, but he wasn't going to let the bounty hunter cut him down. If Big Joe succeeded in killing him, Marlene's life was at risk, too.

The matter was decided for him when the bounty hunter swung a rifle around and leveled it at Marlene.

"Yer a dead woman if'n you don't tell me where that son of a bitch is."

"Put down the rifle, sir," she said. Then Marlene toppled from the driver's box when the bounty hunter fired.

From the report and the huge puff of white smoke, he carried a monster of a gun. Likely a .45-70 H&R Buffalo rifle from the recoil and that he had to reload. Single shot, powerful enough to bring down a man at a thousand yards, the kind of rifle a bounty hunter carried.

Slocum cast a quick look over his shoulder to see how Marlene fared but couldn't find where she had fallen or if she was even alive. The team reared and jerked on the reins he had looped around the wagon brake, making it difficult for him to draw a bead on the bounty hunter. The battle between their fright and the strength of the harness had to end soon. Slocum didn't care which way it went—he needed to get off a shot or Big Joe would have the upper hand.

He dug his toes into the litter in the wagon bed and propelled himself over the tailgate. Slocum hit the ground, rolled, and brought the shotgun up. The bounty hunter watched the rearing team and didn't see Slocum until it was too late. The first shell detonated, lifting the muzzle of the shotgun. Over the years Slocum had developed a sense for when he hit his target and when he missed. This was close.

The bounty hunter jerked about, grabbing for his left side. His rifle fell from his grip as blood oozed between his fingers. He looked up, pure hatred etching his ugly features.

"Slocum!"

Slocum fired the second barrel. He knocked open the breech and ejected both spent shells. Before he had loaded two more shells, he saw there wasn't any need for more gunplay. Big Joe Joseph had caught the second load of buckshot in the chest and was knocked back off his horse. The animal reared, pawed at the air, and then galloped away.

Slocum stood and watched as Big Joe was dragged along behind. His right foot had tangled in the stirrup. After the bounty hunter and his runaway horse disappeared in a cloud of dust, Slocum ran to the wagon, jumped over the traces, and stood on the yoke, taking reins in both hands and pulling hard to settle the team. The horses finally settled down so he could tighten the lash around the wagon brake. Only when it was secured did he hop off on the far side to hunt for Marlene.

He heaved a sigh of relief. The girl sat up in the dust and brushed off the new layers of dirt.

"Are you all right?" He helped her to her feet. Other than the dirt, he saw no trace of blood. Big Joe had either fired for effect or he had been a lousy shot.

"How did he miss at such close range?" She looked at him. "You didn't miss, did you?"

Slocum looked around. He had dropped the shotgun on the far side of the wagon. He shook his head, then reached out to take her hand and lead her back to the driver's box. With a heave, he lifted her off her feet. For a moment, her feet weakly sought purchase, then found a hole in the side of the wagon. She pushed herself on up and sat heavily.

Her response was as depleted as Slocum felt. He brought her a dipper of water, took some himself, then secured the water barrel before climbing back to take the reins.

"We can reach the railroad tracks in ten or fifteen minutes," he said, snapping the reins and steering the team toward the gleaming steel rails. "The repair crew has to be sent anytime now."

"We might have missed them." Although she looked ahead without turning her head, she jerked her thumb back in the direction of the Colorado River. "They can be back there."

"We push on," he said.

"Because of the bounty hunter? Because he might be at the head of a posse?"

Her question hit close to home. Slocum remembered the posse after him. By now they had all gone home. But Big Joe might be only the first of a string of bounty hunters since the reward had been set so high. If he had a way to do so, Slocum would turn himself in for the reward. As it was, getting Marlene back to her family would bring him as much and let him ride off a thousand miles away from all the trouble in San Diego. He had never cared much for San Antonio, but right now it drew him like a flower attracts a bee.

Wheels rattling over the rugged ground, he followed the tracks so long that he wondered if he would drive over the edge of the world before he found the repair crew. The sun sank behind the wagon and still he drove on until a glint ahead made him sit a little straighter. He glanced over at Marlene. She slumped, then said, "I saw it, too. That's the Yuma Bullet ahead."

"Why isn't it running?"

"It might have brought the repair crew out and is parked."

Slocum tried to keep her talking. He preferred even obvious answers to her silence, but too soon Marlene fell back into a glum, mute state.

As they drove closer, he saw the Yuma Bullet had pulled onto a siding. Mad Tom, his fireman, and a burly man in a conductor's uniform stood by the front wheels, arguing. Even when Slocum came within a dozen yards, he didn't disturb their heated debate.

"Tom!" He stood and called. "Good of you to wait for us."

"Damnation, it's Doc Slocum and the little lady herself." He pushed past the conductor and came over. "I wondered if I'd ever see you again, but I shoulda knowed you was too cussed to die."

"Miss Burlison!" The conductor stepped up but hesitated when he heard a shriek of joy.

The outcry from the Pullman car platform told Slocum everyone knew they had arrived.

"Miss Mulligan," he said, touching the brim of his hat. Dust cascaded down. "I brought her back."

For an instant, the girl stared up at him. Then she laughed in delight and called, "You mean you brought Miss Burlison back! I misunderstood."

"She's in bad shape. Terrible things happened to her." Slocum reached out to Marlene to help her down from the wagon. She jerked away from him and climbed down on her own.

Sarah Jane threw her arms around her mistress, but Marlene pushed away from her, too.

"Stop that. Stop that now. Come with me," Sarah Jane said sharply.

"Treat her real gentle," Slocum said, his eyes boring down on Sarah Jane. "She's been through hell."

"You don't tell me what to do," Sarah Jane said sharply.

"Uh, Slocum, I reckon you got a fine story to tell. Let the ladies go off to the Pullman. I need some advice from you on a matter." Mad Tom sounded frantic that he obey.

Slocum had been through too much to argue. He watched as Sarah Jane led Marlene to the Pullman car, all lit up with gaslights. Once inside, Sarah Jane spun Marlene around and poked her in the chest with a finger, backing the woman up.

"That's not right. I'm going to stop that," Slocum said. Tom caught his arm.

"We got some serious problems, Slocum. You let them be. The ways of the rich ain't ours to meddle in."

Sarah Jane closed curtains so he could no longer see how she badgered Marlene. Maybe in her distraught state, someone taking charge was the best thing for Marlene. It still rankled seeing the girl bullied like that after she had almost lost her life a dozen times since the cars fell into the river.

"Why'd you park at this siding? Waiting for us to show up?"

Mad Tom snorted like steam from his locomotive's stack.

"Ain't a bit of it. Fact is, we'd've plowed right on ahead if the ole engine hadn't seized up." He took Slocum's elbow and steered him to where the conductor stood, glaring. "That there's Hanks. Picked him up in Yuma to replace Jefferson."

"That's a hard man to replace."

"He don't even come close," Tom said under his breath. "You shake hands with this one, you count yer fingers

'terwards. Ain't sayin' he's a sneak thief or nuthin' like
at, mind you, but you jist watch out for him."

Hanks walked up to Slocum and gave him the once-over.
was mutual. Taking into account what Tom had said col-
ed Slocum's reaction to the new conductor. The man stood
s tall as Slocum and looked to be as wiry. He had the build
f a man used to long days in the saddle, and his weathered
ace doubled down on that notion. Men who spend their days
nd nights on trains had a different look. Other than phy-
que, conductors prided themselves on their uniforms.
Hanks's fit like he had taken it off a dead man, tight in the
houlders and floppy around the waist.

"You lose your pocket watch?" Slocum asked.

"What's that?"

"You're the first conductor I ever saw who didn't have a
watch tucked away to be sure the train left the station on
ime."

Hanks pressed his gnarled hand against his empty watch
pocket.

"Musta left it with the rest of my gear. You're Slocum,
he one this old walleyed fool is always goin' on about?"

"The name's Slocum. I don't know about the rest."

Hanks gave him a sour look, then said, "You work for
Burlison. Order the engineer to get us on to Deming."

"Because I'm the engineer of the Yuma Bullet's why I
ain't pressin' on," Mad Tom said. His lips thinned, showing
yellowed teeth behind his chapped lips. "We got ourselves
a problem. No oil. If I don't get plenty on the bearings,
they'll seize up and ruin the whole damned engine."

"You don't know what yer talkin' 'bout," Hanks said.
"Them bearings always run hot and stink to high heaven."

"I kin lubricate 'em with your brains," Tom said, "but
them bearings'd be jist as dry as they are now." He pointedly turned his back on the conductor and faced Slocum.
"We need oil to get into a repair depot. No train's comin' this
way from Deming until we git back. And none's comin'

across the bridge anytime soon. The repair crew foreman tole me it'd be at least a week to rebuild."

"So we sit and wait a week?"

"Well, Slocum, might not have to. See, there's an abandoned town a half-dozen miles off that might have stored up some oil."

"A railroad town?" Slocum asked.

"Made strictly to house the construction crews. A thrivin' mee-tropolis in its day, but it got abandoned when it warn't needed no more."

"Any water there?"

"Nary a drop," Tom said. "The depots along the way where we fill up have a handful of folks tendin' 'em. That ain't one."

"You want me to ride on over and see if I can rustle up some oil? How much do you need?"

"A gallon would do me, but less if that's all there is. You got a wagon. Don't matter how much there is 'cuz you kin load it all up fer me."

Slocum wanted nothing more than to curl up in a quiet corner and sleep for a week. He had more aches and bruises than any five men ought to sport.

"Get me some victuals and water and I'll be on my way. Six miles away, you say?"

"Might be more. Could be ten. I'd have set out myself but crossin' this desert on foot's enough to kill a man."

"Heard that's the case," Slocum said. Memory of his own hike through the desert would haunt him for a spell. "You want to help get the water into the wagon?" He looked straight at Hanks, who pointedly turned away.

"He's like that, Slocum," Mad Tom said. "Me and the coal boy'll help." Louder so Hanks could hear, he added, "Some folks on this here railroad are used to workin' fer their pay."

The trio poured water from the train into the barrel, made sure the team had plenty to drink, and then Slocum stepped up into the driver's box. He cast a quick look up at the Pullman car, worrying about the way Sarah Jane had acted toward Marlene. Shrugging this off, he settled down, took the reins, and snapped them. The team began pulling.

He had gone barely a mile when he hit a rock that set the entire wagon to bouncing. He fought to keep control, then he went cold inside.

From the rear of the wagon came muffled curses. He touched his six-gun, then remembered the Colt was empty. Reaching back, he found the knife he had taken off one of the men he had killed in the desert, then swung around, grabbed a mattress, and yanked it away. He thrust out the knife, ready to spit whoever was hiding.

He drew back as Sarah Jane looked up and smiled.

"It's about time you realized you had a traveling companion. Aren't you going to invite me to sit up there with you?"

Slocum fought to find words but couldn't. He sank back and shook his head in wonder. Taking the job to see Marlene Burlison safely to San Antonio was going to be the death of him yet.

15

"What are you doing? Don't go back. I forbid it!" Sarah Jane grabbed his arm and dug in her fingernails until she drew blood. Slocum pulled away.

"I just spent the past few days babysitting your mistress. That's not something I'm looking forward to doing with you."

"Oh, John, really? This isn't a dangerous trip, is it? If it is, I'm sure you'll keep me safe and sound." She snuggled close until Slocum felt their mingled sweat plastering his sleeve to his arm. "I got so bored sitting around, waiting, with nothing to do. I simply *had* to get away."

"Miss Burlison needs you," he said. "She's been through more than you can imagine."

"Really? Then tell me about it. Every little detail. I want to hear it all! What did she say about me?"

Slocum wondered what kind of servant Sarah Jane was. She had lived it up in the Pullman car while her mistress almost drowned, got raped by a gang of savages, fought Indians, and was damned near shot by a bounty hunter. Then the elements had been brutal, offering too little water and too much heat.

"She can tell you."

"I want *you* to, John. Now."

He started to turn the team around, but Sarah Jane pouted and drew away from him.

"Oh, be like that. Why you won't tell me is a great mystery."

"It's none of your business, unless Miss Burlison wants to tell you. Did you ask her?"

"I did. Her lips were too chapped and her tongue too swollen for her to speak."

"All the more reason for you to be tending her and not riding to a ghost town with me."

"I remember the town," she said. "We passed through it a few times as the tracks were being laid. Hell on Wheels, they called it. Nobody would escort me into the town to see what it had to offer and . . . and Marlene refused to go. Such a spoilsport."

Slocum had been in enough boomtowns to guess what a railroad town—and a temporary one moving along with the tracks as they were laid—could be like. It was no place for a lady and her maid, though he had been surprised at Sarah Jane's appetites in San Diego at the whorehouse and even more amazed that Marlene had allowed her to indulge them.

"Rough trade," he said. "But if you passed through, tell me where the building crew stored its oil."

"I don't know, but there were a couple big warehouses not far from the tracks. I saw them from the window of my car as . . . as Mr. Burlison did whatever business he had to at the main station house."

Slocum doubted finding the storage area would be difficult. At most, only a few hundred people had occupied the town, and all of them were transients. A couple tent saloons, a hotel or two, and more likely bunkhouses, a company store, and whatever else the town needed to survive.

"All supplies were brought in?"

"By rail, of course, you silly goose. There wasn't any

water, and who would raise cattle or grow crops out here?" Sarah Jane made a sweeping gesture encompassing the entire desert. Slocum saw that her nails had been perfectly manicured. Comparing them with the way Marlene's hands looked after a few days of roughing it made him a tad resentful.

"Did you get all the way to Deming and then return to find us—to find Marlene?"

"Marlene, is it? You and she are on first name terms now? Was it charming out there, just the two of you? Under the stars?"

"Under the killing hot sun without water most of the time, and when we did have water, Marlene almost drowned after her Pullman car toppled into the Colorado from the trestle." He felt a knot grow in his belly. "Jefferson died, too, trying to save her."

"Oh, we picked up a new conductor in Yuma. I don't know a thing about him, but he is rather cute."

"His uniform doesn't fit," Slocum said. Why that bothered him had to be considered some other day. Ahead through the heat shimmer popped up a tall building. He pointed it out.

"That's a bell tower. I don't know why Mr. Burlison ever had it built. Such a waste of time and money."

"Might be he likes bells."

"Do you like belles, John? Of course you do. We spent a fine time together, and I am certainly a belle."

"The belle of the ball," he said.

"I hope I'm the belle of *your* ball." She reached over and grabbed at his crotch. "I'd certainly like to ring these balls again."

He caught her wrist and moved her hand away.

"There's someone else in town."

"What? How could there be? This is railroad property. They're trespassing! You're just saying that to distract me. Who would be here? Other than the two of us?"

Slocum wondered at her outrage, but the solitary mule hitched beside the tumbledown hotel warned of at least one other man in town. The mule wore a double pack fastened with a diamond hitch the way a prospector would sling his gear. They drove past with Sarah Jane not even looking up to see the animal and what it meant.

"That big warehouse where railroad supplies were kept?" He pointed to a two-story windowless building down the street from the hotel.

"It was. Are you sure someone else is in town? What are you going to do about him, John? He can't stay. I won't allow it!"

"Why's it up to you to tell him where he can get out of the sun?"

"I am the representative of the S&P and as such must uphold the integrity of all property along the tracks. He might be stealing something valuable."

"The only thing of value out here," Slocum said, "is water. Right now, I'd swap him some for a small barrel of oil so we can get the Yuma Bullet rolling again."

"Yes, I want that," Sarah Jane said. "You track down that interloper and get from him what you need. Don't be afraid to shoot him either, if the need arises. If there even is someone else here. I feel so all alone—with you." She laid her head on his shoulder and closed her eyes.

"Now that's real kind of you to give me permission to kill a man." Slocum shoved his feet down hard against the front of the driver's box and half stood, using his weight as well as his strength to halt the team.

Sarah Jane let out a tiny sound of disgust at having her headrest move so abruptly. She sat up and stared at the warehouse as if it had interrupted her doing something important. From the way she acted, Slocum doubted she believed him when he said someone else was roaming around the abandoned town.

The warehouse door had fallen off its hinges. Inside he

heard small animals moving around, staying out of the fierce sun until the desert cooled off. There was no telling what else he might find inside.

"Stay in the back of the wagon," he told Sarah Jane. Slocum hefted the shotgun, then jumped to the ground.

She protested but obeyed. He couldn't figure her out. She was too many contradictions all rolled up into one lovely package for him to understand. For all that, Marlene Burlison proved a mystery, too, but he found himself worrying about her back at the train more than he did about Sarah Jane's safety in what had been a ghost town but now was inhabited by at least one prospector.

It might be as easy as Sarah Jane said, though. After all, he had her permission to cut down whoever sought out a bit of shade in this fierce desert.

He stepped over the fallen door and pressed his back against the inside wall until his eyes adjusted to the dimmer light. All the tools had been taken as well as most of the supplies. A few crates had been spilled onto the ground. Picking up the contents must have been harder than replacing whatever had been stored. He gingerly picked his way through the debris, using the barrel of his shotgun to push away discarded junk. When he found a small gallon-sized cask, he pounced on it.

Reading what had been written on the side proved difficult in the dim light, but he made out two letters: IL. He tapped the side of the cask with the shotgun butt and grinned when he realized the cask was full. Slinging the shotgun over his shoulder, he bent, grabbed, and lifted the barrel. It sloshed about a little, but when he carried it to the doorway, he saw the missing letter was a faded O.

He swung the cask up onto his shoulder and went to the rear of the wagon. Sarah Jane had stretched out on the thin mattress and slept peacefully swaddled by the heat. He lowered the oil keg and secured it in the wagon, then considered waking her. They had found what they needed. Returning to the Yuma Bullet as soon as possible would get the train steaming along to San Antonio.

But he wondered about the prospector. Other than alkali dust, there wasn't a whale of a lot to dig up in this area. Toward the southwest, Bisbee and Tombstone, was the place to hunt for silver and copper. He doubted this stretch of the Sonoran Desert yielded much in the way of coal or other minerals valuable to the railroad.

Slocum cursed under his breath as he touched the shotgun barrel. The few minutes it had been in the sun had heated it more than if he had been firing it steadily. He sucked on his burned finger, then realized this did little good when his mouth was dry. He took the time to swallow a dipper of water from the wagon's supply before setting out to find the man sharing the nameless town with him and Sarah Jane.

The mule stood patiently in the same spot. The shade made the wait for its master easier, but the sharp, hot wind whipping up over the desert made the spot less agreeable than inside the building, out of the wind and sun.

Slocum chanced a look around the door into the hotel lobby. He stepped inside quickly, then stood stock-still to listen. The only sound he could hear was the whistling of the wind through cracks in the walls. Slocum continued his hunt through the empty hotel, thinking the prospector had come here to die. As many desert varmints as he saw, none of them were the scavengers that would be intent on a freshly dead body. From the look of the mule, the prospector hadn't been here very long.

He stepped out the back door and looked along the line of dilapidated buildings. A vacant lot littered with empty bottles gave mute testimony to where the saloon had been. Pitch a tent, drop a board over a couple sawhorses, and the ginmill was open for business. The building just beyond had likely been one of the whorehouses. A town like this could support more than one saloon and certainly more than one house of ill repute. Railroad workers got thirsty and horny, with little else to keep them distracted from their backbreaking labor.

He took a couple steps toward the whorehouse when he heard the sound of a shovel digging into hard ground. Slocum stepped back into the hotel and peered around the doorframe in time to see a short man with a huge handlebar mustache come out of the next building. The man walked fast, as if he was late. But late for what? He almost ran past Slocum and fetched the mule. By the time he led the pack animal back, Slocum had slipped deeper into the shadows to avoid being seen.

The prospector had found something but what it might be posed a question that burned at Slocum's curiosity bump as fiercely as the sun hammered down on his head. Matters got more complicated when the prospector led the mule away from the buildings. Slocum waited until he disappeared over a rise before following to spy.

He flopped onto his belly and peeked over the top of a sand dune to see the prospector kick down a whitewashed picket fence around a grave. The grizzled old man had gone to the town cemetery to desecrate it. He kicked and stomped, reached down, and pulled away crude grave markers and finally stopped when he reached an opened grave. Slocum froze when the prospector took a look around, to see if anyone watched his trespass.

Slocum almost laughed out loud. He wanted to stand and yell out that by the order of one Miss Sarah Jane Mulligan, the prospector was guilty of trespass and, as such, could be gunned down in the name of the S&P Railroad. Then Slocum stilled as he saw the prospector drop to his knees and begin hauling out leather bags that looked like those used by banks to transfer gold coins.

Three leather bags came from the grave to rest on the edge of the hole. Slocum had thought the prospector had found this grave already open, then realized from the look of the soil that he had opened it before going to the whorehouse to poke around there. He wanted a new hiding place ready before fetching these bags.

Slocum caught his breath when the prospector opened one bag and held up a gold coin, which flashed and gleamed in the sunlight. The man stuffed a handful of coins into a jacket pocket before lacing up the leather sack again. With a grunt loud enough for Slocum to hear it plainly, the prospector heaved the sack up and onto the back of the mule. The animal protested. Then it protested with an even louder braying when two more sacks joined the first.

Knowing where the man intended to go, Slocum backtracked and waited hidden inside the hotel. Less than five minutes passed before the slowly moving mule, led by its master, went directly to the side of the whorehouse. The wind whirled up tiny dust devils. Any tracks left by the mule's hooves would be erased in minutes.

The prospector transferred the three sacks inside the building. Slocum caught the sound of more shoveling, and twenty minutes later the prospector came out, looked around, then led his mule away, going due east. Slocum remained hidden for some time, thinking about what he had just seen. The prospector had somehow discovered the gold hidden in the cemetery and had done what he could to make it appear that vandals had desecrated the graves and had stumbled on the contents. Whoever had first buried the gold wouldn't believe that, but confusion had to be a valuable tool in the old prospector's arsenal.

He might have seen the robbers bury it or could even be one of the gang intent on double-crossing the rest. Whatever the truth, Slocum wanted to see if all three sacks contained gold coins. With the sun sinking fast behind him, he went to the whorehouse and poked his head around to be certain it was as deserted as he believed. It was as empty as a whore's promise.

Walking carefully to avoid leaving boot prints in the

drifted dust along the corridor opening into a dozen cribs, he hunted for any trace of the prospector. The sneak thief had covered his tracks well, but one crib caught Slocum's eye. Initials had been carved into the door long enough back for the wood to dry out and splinter. A greasy smear across the initials was fresh, as if the prospector had run his finger over them while he remembered better days—or nights.

Slipping into the small room without leaving a track proved difficult, and Slocum soon gave up the attempt. An old broom was lying on the floor, and he figured that the prospector had used it to sweep away his own tracks. Bolder now, Slocum looked around the room. Reaching out let him place his palms on either wall. The length was hardly six feet but a pallet had been spread to fill most of the floor space. He poked at it and then saw how a thin layer of dirt covered a plank. He ran his fingers around, found a knothole, and tugged.

The former occupant of this crib had dug a shallow hole to keep her money and precious belongings. A tawdry piece of costume jewelry, broken in half, rested in the crude vault. A gold chain had been dropped on top of it, but Slocum cared nothing about that. Three leather sacks filled most of the cavity.

A quick check assured him he had been right about the contents. There had to be a thousand dollars or more in gold and silver coins. Rubbing at the dirt on one bag revealed faded letters. A bank in Deming had lost a considerable amount of cash. Grunting with effort, he heaved the sacks from the hole, then carefully replaced the plank and swept dirt over it until even his sharp eye detected no difference between before he'd found the cache and now that was empty.

He tied the leather laces together and staggered a mite as he slung them over his shoulder and stood. Being this rich ought to have given his step all the energy necessary to lightly walk out, but he had been through too much in recent days for that. A week recovering would put him right.

Using the same care he had when he refitted the wooden lid, he swept away all traces that he had been there. In the narrow corridor, he ran his own finger over the carved initials.

"Who're RV and PC?" he asked in a low voice. He had no idea but this spot marked a veritable gold mine for him, even if the coins had been stolen.

Brushing his way clear of the whorehouse, he turned toward the warehouse and the wagon, where he had left Sarah Jane. She hadn't come for him, so he guessed she still slept. As he made his way, he looked for a different hiding spot.

The best he could do was a depression under a pile of rocks. He needed a shovel to dig, and that would have taken more time than he had since the earth was as hard as a brick. The rocks provided an easy marker, and he doubted anyone would blunder by and want to remove the rocks when there were hundreds all around. These were simply stacked. Otherwise, they were ordinary.

He nestled the leather sacks down and took his time placing the rocks over them. When he was sure no trace of the leather showed, he dumped handfuls of sand over the pile until it disappeared. When he'd finished, he sat back and wiped away what traces he had left, though the rising wind did a better job than he ever could.

The idea that he should have taken a few coins as the prospector had occurred to him, but something warned him against being too greedy. He had a pile of gold and silver waiting for him when he returned. That might be a week or a year, but it would be his for the taking then.

He got to the wagon and peered into the back as Sarah Jane stirred, stretched, and arched her back, nicely showing off her breasts. Like a cat, she rolled over and stretched again, this time putting on a show for him.

"It's dark. I hadn't meant to sleep so long."

"It's the heat," he said. "It makes you sleepy. You wouldn't have slept this long if you hadn't needed it."

"I'm all rested," she said in a seductive voice. She unfastened the top button of her blouse. "How about some exercise to get the blood racing?" As she worked on the next button, Slocum held up his hand to silence her.

"What is it?" She scrambled over to him on her knees and stuck her head out.

Distant angry cries caught on the wind. A gunshot came. Then a volley, as if a battle was being fought.

"It's time for us to get the hell out of here. This might be a ghost town but whoever's doing all the shooting's no ghost."

"Am I in danger?"

"Not if we make tracks now."

Slocum climbed into the driver's box. Sarah Jane joined him. Her hand shook in fear as he swung the team around and headed back along the railroad tracks toward the stranded Yuma Bullet. Being quit of the town suited him just fine. Somehow, not taking Sarah Jane up on her sexy offer suited him, too.

He had been in the hot sun too long, he decided.

16

"It was ever so exciting. Why, Miss Burlison, let me tell you all about my adventures." Sarah Jane took Marlene by the arm and steered her to the Pullman car in what Slocum thought was a most unladylike bum's rush.

He stared at the two, wondering how they got on when no one else was around to overhear. His speculation was cut short when Mad Tom came up and grabbed his arm to spin him around.

"You danged fool! You shouldna took her out like that! Mr. Burlison would have your hide nailed to the barn door fer doin' that."

"I got the oil. You want to open the keg and see if it's all right or do you want to stand here and complain about something that's over and done?"

"Yer a complete fool, Slocum. Crazy from the sun? You kin always tell the boss that when he calls you on it."

Slocum saw the two girls in their Pullman, arguing. The windows, in spite of the heat, were closed, and he couldn't hear a word that was being said, but Marlene gestured wildly and turned red in the face. She spun and started to walk away but Sarah Jane grabbed her and the two of them started their argument all over again.

"Catfights ain't worth spyin' on. 'Specially not 'tween the two of them. They's like sisters in some sense I never did fathom. That the oil?" Mad Tom elbowed Slocum away from the wagon and grabbed the cask. With a single heave, he had it out of the wagon. "Danged if it ain't. Even the brand I use."

Slocum had to laugh. The only oil likely to be stored was whatever S&P used in all their locomotives.

"Open it up. I didn't want to tap the keg for fear of ruining the oil inside."

"Might be ruined from the heat," Tom said. "But it ain't. Smells sweet and good, jist what I need to keep that bearing all shiny and spinning." He heaved the cask up and wrapped his arms around it, carrying it as he would a small child.

Slocum followed and watched as Tom and his fireman poured the oil into their long-spouted can and began liberally applying it to the front wheel bearings. Most of the cask was gone by the time Tom finished, stepped back, and put his hands on his hips in satisfaction.

"The ole Bullet'll roll like new now, thanks to you, Slocum."

The entire drive back in the wagon had given Slocum new worries about the gold and silver he had hidden. The gunfire told him the coins—*his* loot—wasn't as secure as he had hoped. With only occasional pilgrims passing by, the cache would go unnoticed. So much gunfire told him the gang was out hunting the prospector or maybe even a posse had come looking for the stolen cash. No matter how far he traveled, he couldn't get away from bank robbers.

The difference before was his innocence. Now he'd hidden money taken from a bank, making him an accomplice in the eyes of the law. For such a treasure trove, he would risk getting caught. He had been through so much up to this point that he felt he deserved it.

"We have to stop in that ghost town," Slocum said.

"Whatever for? I'm highballin' it all the way to Deming."

"As a favor to me. I can get another cask of the oil to be sure you don't run dry."

"They call me Mad Tom but I ain't no man's fool. You got some reason for stoppin' there, don't you, Slocum? Don't make no never mind to me. Climb aboard. Once we build up a head of steam, we can be at that there town in an hour."

Slocum looked at the Pullman car and wished he could ride back there. But whose company did he prefer? He realized it was Marlene's.

Grabbing a handrail, he pulled himself up into the cab and stood out of the way as the fireman began stoking the banked fire while Tom worked the valves and caused a constant hissing sound from the boilers.

"Up to pressure. Stoke, you lazy son of a bitch, stoke!"

With a rebel yell, Tom pulled back on the lever and the Yuma Bullet began to groan. More power caused the wheels to turn, and within a minute they were racing along the track that had taken Slocum hours to cover in the wagon. As good as his word, Tom began slowing when they approached the town. The screech of steel on steel caused the entire train to shudder and shake. Then they ground to a halt not a dozen yards from the warehouse.

"Come on over and look for the oil," Slocum said. "I'll show you where I found it before."

"No need," Tom said. "I 'bout lived in that warehouse when they was buildin' this stretch of the 'road." He clamped down the levers, released steam, and hopped to the ground. He cast a quick look at Slocum and said, "You go do what you gotta do and we'll meet back at the engine."

Slocum wasted no time going to the rock cairn. He stared at it for a moment, wondering if he was doing the right thing retrieving the gold and silver. Leaving it here was as safe as having it in the bank. Then he changed his mind when he heard loud shouts in the distance and more gunfire. He had no idea who sought the leather bags or how willing they would be to cut down anyone with the money.

He kicked away the rocks, hefted the three bags, and staggered along for a couple steps until he got his balance. Then he would have liked to turn tail and run when he heard hooves pounding behind him, coming from the north. He got back to the Yuma Bullet before Tom. The fireman was nowhere to be seen, giving Slocum the chance to find a spot in the coal tender to stash the money bags. As he came back into the cab, he saw who had been riding so hard.

Astride a horse with lathered flanks rode the prospector. He had traded his mule for a saddle horse and had enough ammo to begin dispensing it with wild abandon. A slug ricocheted off the engine's side and whistled away. Slocum reached for his six-shooter, then remembered he had to get more cartridges. But he had the shotgun taken from the wagon. He grabbed it, lifted it to his shoulder, and fired one barrel.

The recoil knocked him back a half pace because he hadn't braced for it. Worse, he remembered he hadn't pocketed any more shells. He had one more chance to stop the prospector.

"You thievin', lily-livered *thief!* That's mine what you took. And I know you took it 'cuz I spied on you."

Slocum leveled the shotgun, took careful aim this time, and made the buckshot count. The prospector grunted and jerked to the side, still in the saddle. But he had dropped his six-gun. He turned his horse and galloped away, letting Slocum climb down from the cab and retrieve the fallen pistol.

He was just in time because the outraged man wasn't running, he was regrouping. He pulled a Henry from a saddle sheath and started firing at Slocum. One or two of the pellets had caught him in the arm, throwing off his aim and making it difficult for him to lever in a new round and fire again. Slocum took a stance, aimed, and fired. The prospector jerked again as the slug hit him. But he was determined and trotted about, trying to get the rifle to bear.

"Git on back here, Slocum. We're leavin' without you if you don't climb aboard! Company policy, we don't shoot it out with no outlaws if we kin outrun 'em."

The Yuma Bullet's steam whistle cut through the air and startled the prospector into missing with his next round. Rather than continue the gunfight, Slocum ran for all he was worth, jumped, and caught the handhold on the cab. He swung around, sat, and looked for another shot.

"Damnation, you got 'em comin' out o' their hill like ants!"

Slocum saw what the engineer meant. A half-dozen men galloped through the town, firing as they came. The bullets *spanged!* off the locomotive's iron sides. And then the train gained speed and the horses fell behind, victims of the heat and exhaustion from such a fierce run to overtake the train. Slocum caught the glint of sunlight off at least one badge.

A posse.

He swung around and saw that the prospector had high-tailed it due south to get away from the lawmen. The posse milled about until the one Slocum pegged as the marshal led them after the fleeing horseman.

"I do declare, it ain't never dull with you around, Slocum," the engineer said. He wiped his face with an oily rag. "From the sound them wheels are makin', it was good advice stoppin' fer more oil. We're gonna need it."

"Don't slow down," Slocum said. He leaned out and took a gander at the tracks behind the train. The riders had disappeared in the dust and distance.

He pulled himself back into the cab and sat on a drop seat. This proved worse than standing. The vibration from the wheels shook him all over. On his feet, his knees took most of the punishment from the rocking, swaying engine. He tried not to look too obvious but could not keep his eyes off the spot where he had stashed the money. If the fireman or Tom discovered the bags, he could buy them off by sharing the loot. The engineer might be called Mad Tom, but he had never heard anyone call him Stupid Tom. Several hundred dollars in gold coins would be quite an enticing reward for keeping his mouth shut.

"I'll be glad to get on down to San Antonio," Tom said. "I'm gettin' sick of drivin' Miss Burlison around."

"She's a mighty fine-looking woman," Slocum said.

"If you like the type," Tom replied. "She's not our kind, like me and you, Slocum. Her pa tried to raise her so she wasn't all snooty and stuck up, but you see how she turned out. Then again, might be you don't care, the way you and her have been runnin' off all the time."

"I wouldn't call it running off," Slocum said. "Fate's thrown us together. Ever since I fetched her and Sarah Jane from a"—he bit off the description of the maid spying on a couple screwing their brains out—"from a tight spot in San Diego."

"Sarah Jane," Tom said, his eyes going distant. "Now there's a fine woman, but you know that. You and her done spent so much time together, you savin' her life and all."

"That's the start of a tall tale," Slocum said. "I can't say I saved her from anything much."

"Bullets were flyin' and men was huntin' you two down."

"The posse," Slocum said, wanting to look at the tracks behind them again. He realized how guilty this made him look, but Tom didn't know they had outrun a posse. For all he knew, the men shooting at them were robbers.

"What's that whistling noise?" Slocum stood and looked forward. "You sprung a leak in the boiler. There's a plume of steam coming from the side."

"Damnation, you're right. We're losin' pressure. Ain't much so far, but we can't keep up this pace and hope to reach Deming in one piece. We're still five–six hours away, and that's at top speed."

"Better to limp along and keep moving than to blow a rivet," Slocum said, thinking how determined the posse had to be. They had ridden the entire way from Deming, where the bank had been robbed. How long they had been scouring the desert for the robbers—and the stolen loot—was a question he needed to answer. The longer the posse had been out on the trail, the more determined they'd be to bring the robbers to justice.

With so much gold and silver coinage at stake, the reward had to be considerable.

"I reckon I ought to go pay my respects to Miss Burlison," Slocum said. There wasn't any more to do here as the train chugged along.

"If that's what you call it now, go on. Jist don't get caught." Mad Tom laughed and slapped Slocum on the back.

Slocum made his way along the tender, wondering if Tom or the fireman would find the gold. What they did then depended on how honest they were. If they had the morals of a railroad bull, splitting the gold with them or even giving it away would end the problem. Honest men would be harder to deal with since they would turn him in to the Deming marshal.

Slocum swung around and landed on the platform between cars. He considered knocking but there was little reason to do so. The sound of the wheels drowned out any such polite noise. He opened the door and went inside, immediately aware something was wrong.

Marlene sat facing away from him. She didn't move as he made his way toward her. Then he caught her reflection in a mirror mounted on the rear wall of the car. Her eyes were closed and her mouth slack. She wasn't sleeping; she was unconscious. As he came even with her, he saw movement out the rear door. Tending the boss's daughter should have taken priority over everything else, but she was in no immediate danger.

Sarah Jane was.

She struggled with the conductor, pushing him away, only to have him grab her and whirl her around to get a choke hold intended to subdue her. Slocum slammed the door open as hard as he could. Hanks either had to release Sarah Jane and hang on to the handrail or go tumbling to the ground. Even at the Yuma Bullet's leisurely twenty miles an hour, such an impact would do more than clack his teeth together.

Sarah Jane sat, gasping for breath and clutching her throat. Slocum saw Hanks reach under his left arm. The wind flapped his ill-fitting coat open to reveal a shoulder rig and small pistol hidden there.

Instinct rather than thought drove Slocum's fist to the side of Hanks's head. The conductor jerked away, got his pistol out, but was facing in the wrong direction. Slocum grabbed him by the seat of his pants and the back of his coat and heaved as hard as he could. The man sailed through the air. From the way he landed headfirst, he wouldn't bedevil Sarah Jane again. Or anyone else. Slocum was sure he had killed the conductor.

"What was going on?" He helped her to her feet.

"I, he, he tried to kidnap me!"

Slocum looked back into the Pullman car, where Marlene Burlison slumped against the side of the car, still unconscious.

"He won't bother you again. And I doubt he intended to kidnap you when Miss Burlison would make for better ransom."

"Why, yes, of course," Sarah Jane said. Flustered, she pushed past him into the Pullman. She hesitated when she saw Marlene, then went to the girl's side. "Get some water for her, John. There's a pitcher up front."

Slocum saw the small rack with glasses and a fancy painted porcelain pitcher. He poured a glass and brought it back. Marlene was awake and looking frightened. She stared up at him and started to speak, but Sarah Jane cut her off.

"John saved us, Marlene. He saved us."

"But I—" The blonde took the glass and clutched it in both hands, still spilling a fair amount as she drank.

"I'll thank him for you, Marlene. You rest up from your ordeal."

"This has gone too far," Marlene said, shaking her head. She took another sip of the water to wet her whistle. "We've got to tell him—"

"This has been such a shock to your system. I'll deal with it for you." Sarah Jane pushed Slocum toward the rear of the car and said in a low voice, "Poor thing is overcome by the kidnap attempt."

"He tried to kidnap you, not her," Slocum said.

"I drew his attention away from her. That was a mistake, I know, but I kept him from harming her. From Miss Burlison."

"That was mighty brave of you," Slocum said, looking from the dark-haired woman to where Marlene clung to the now empty glass as if her life depended on it. "You decoyed him away?"

"Why, yes, that's what I did."

"A kidnapper ought to know who he's sent to snatch."

"The heat, everything is so confused," Sarah Jane said. "Let's not worry our heads about it. I'll go look after her. You ride with the engineer. Marlene is distraught enough and shouldn't engage in conversation for a while."

Slocum let her herd him forward and push him out of the car. He made his way back to the engine cab.

"What went on back there? I heard a shot and thought I saw Hanks jump from the train."

"Nothing to worry about," Slocum said. "I just lightened the load a mite." The engineer could nurse the train along to the depot. Slocum would do all the worrying about Marlene Burlison and how close a kidnapper had come to successfully spiriting her away.

17

"Don't be silly. It's safe, John." Sarah Jane clung to his arm and laid her head on his shoulder. "This is an S&P town."

"That conductor—Hanks—got hired on here, dead-headed to Yuma, and then tried to kidnap Marlene. It wasn't chance. Her pa's enemies sent him. I'd bet money on that."

Sarah Jane stirred uneasily and clung more tenaciously to him. The day was cooler than previous ones because of clouds scudding in from over the Pelonsilla Mountains to the southwest, but any chance of rain cooling the stifling heat even more was slim. Slocum moved away enough to let air circulate between him and the girl.

"Mr. Burlison has enemies everywhere."

"That's why he hired me to look after Marlene." Slocum looked around uneasily. Being so far from the Pullman car, where Marlene took a siesta during the afternoon heat, reminded him how he had almost failed her.

That worry festered into something more he couldn't quite figure out. Since pulling into Deming, Sarah Jane had done all she could to keep him away from the woman he had been hired to protect. Mad Tom worked to fix the boiler on the Yuma Bullet, but it had been a day already and might be another before repairs were completed for the final run across New Mexico and down the western border of Texas following the newly completed S&P tracks.

"You're doing a fine job of it. She couldn't be happier. And safer."

"When we got to the depot, there were only two other engines here. Now there are eight. The Yuma Bullet has held up traffic going west."

"I heard a train coming from the west last night. The Colorado River bridge must be fixed."

"I didn't hear anything." He tensed. Any train coming from the direction of Yuma might bring a posse with it. And the one out in the desert where the prospector had fought off the lawmen from Deming had plenty of time to reach a depot with a telegraph.

He wished he hadn't stashed the gold in the engine. When Tom and his fireman had gotten to serious work on the locomotive boiler, he had removed a steel plate in the tender's wall and stuffed the three sacks of coins in a recess. With the plate bolted back into place, the entire train had to be dismantled to find it. Still, getting caught with the stolen money meant a noose for him. If the Deming marshal bothered to inquire, San Dismas would reply that he was wanted there, too.

The sooner he got to San Antonio and lit out across the Texas prairie on horseback, the safer he would be.

"I need some things for the trip," Sarah Jane said.

"Send one of the depot employees," he said, not wanting to leave Marlene unguarded. More than that, he had a gut-wrenching fear he would be recognized. Staying in the rail yard was the best thing he could do to avoid the town marshal.

"Oh, John, you can be so ignorant. These are things for Marlene, and I have to pick them out. She *needs* them for the trip."

"She can wait until San Antonio."

"Now, now," Sarah Jane said sternly. "You will accompany me into town to buy what I—we—need."

"I need to talk to the engineer. Wait here." Slocum saw a flare of defiance that died quickly.

"Hurry, John. You don't want me to get bored and wander off on my own. What would Marlene say if you let me go unescorted into such a dingy frontier town as this?"

He barely heard. He called to Mad Tom and asked, "How long before the boiler's fixed up?"

"Another hour, maybe two. We got to hook up four passenger cars, a mail car, and a caboose."

"What? Why? Burlison said this was an express intended to get his daughter to San Antonio as fast as possible."

"The traffic in both directions done got screwed up with the bridge goin' down the way it did. With the Yuma Bullet pluggin' up traffic, too, well, we were as responsible fer the bottleneck as anything. The dispatcher's workin' hisself into a dither tryin' to get all caught up."

"A train came in last night?"

"Early mornin', actually. It's already steamin' on down into Texas. I tried to convince the dispatcher to couple on Miss Burlison's car, but her pa said no. He's burnin' up the telegraph wires with instructions. He trusts me and the Yuma Bullet to get her home safe 'n' sound, not some other walleyed, drunk son-of-a-bitch engineer."

"I'm going into town."

"You escortin' her?"

"We'll be back before you pull out."

"Won't—can't—leave without you and her. 'Specially her. But don't go dallyin' none." A loud crash made Tom turn and shake his head. "What's with you buzzards? You all born stupid and with ten thumbs?" He went to help lift a large curved plate into place.

Slocum saw that this was the final piece. Once it was riveted on, the Yuma Bullet need only build up steam and pull out. Already the additional cars were being attached.

Sarah Jane tapped her foot impatiently when he got back to her.

"Took you long enough," she said. "Now, the first place I want to go is the dress shop on the plaza. The last time we were through, they took measurements and should have a dress ready."

She chattered on as Slocum walked beside her, looking about suspiciously. She jerked him to a halt in front of a bookstore.

"Oh, I must see if they have anything new to read. I finished that Mark Twain book."

Slocum started to say he would wait outside, in spite of the heat, when he saw someone down the street that made him reach for his six-shooter. The first thing he had done after arriving in Deming had been to take his Colt Navy to a gunsmith, have it repaired, oiled, and loaded with fresh rounds. His foresight paid off now.

"What's wrong?"

"The prospector," Slocum said. "The one from the ghost town. That's him. He must have been on the train that arrived this morning."

"Are you sure?" Sarah Jane squinted. "I can't be certain, but then I never got a good look at him."

"We're going back and—"

"We're doing no such thing. I am going to peruse the new titles, then we will pick up the dresses."

"Look at your books. I'll do the rest of your errands."

Sarah Jane looked amused. "You? Going to a ladies' dress store?"

"Or we go back."

She sniffed, stood on tiptoe, and gave him a quick peck on the cheek before bustling into the bookstore. Slocum wasted no time going after the prospector. The man was as tenacious as the bounty hunter had been, but with better reason. All that gold could convince a man to circle the world and then some.

Slocum crossed the plaza and sought the man, but when he reached the general store where he had spotted the prospector, he had disappeared. Slocum stepped into the cool interior and looked around. The clerk dozed behind the counter. The prospector hadn't come in here. Slocum backed out and wondered if the man had gone into a saloon—or had seen him and now became the hunter.

One place the prospector wouldn't go was the marshal's office down a street leading off the far side of the plaza. Slocum eliminated possibilities one by one and came up empty. He went to the dress store, stared at the two dresses in the window, using the plate glass reflection to watch the street behind him. Mistaking another man for the prospector was a possibility, but Slocum doubted that had happened. The best he could hope for was the man not sighting his quarry.

"Can I help you, sir? You seem quite taken by the window mannequins. If you are looking for some companionship, there are other places in town you can go."

"Sorry, ma'am," he said, touching the brim of his Stetson to the clerk. "I was sent to pick up a dress."

"For your wife?"

"For Marlene Burlison. Or her maid, I suppose. Sarah Jane Mulligan."

"Oh, Miss Burlison! I had expected her days ago. Step inside. I'll fetch the dresses."

Slocum felt uneasy inside the shop and even more so when the clerk returned with three large boxes.

"If there is anything more to tailor, have Miss Burlison drop by."

Slocum touched his coat pocket. He had replaced the dirty, ripped finery provided by Morgan Burlison with more durable clothing from the rail yard crew's supplies. Not taking even one gold coin from his stash now came back to haunt him.

"I don't have the money to pay for these."

"Oh, these are for Miss Burlison. I'll put them on her bill

and send it to her father. I'm sure Mr. Burlison will pay promptly. He has in the past when Miss Burlison lacked funds."

"Thanks, ma'am," Slocum said. "It would be a problem to fetch the money since we're pulling out in a few minutes."

"Then you must hurry. I do hope Miss Burlison will let me know if these suit her. She is such a good customer and always stops in whenever she is traveling this way."

Slocum wrestled the large cardboard boxes about, trying to keep his gun hand free and realizing that wasn't going to happen. He returned to the bookstore just as Sarah Jane came out with a small bundle of books neatly wrapped in brown paper and tied with string.

"Oh, my dresses! I must look at them!"

"On the train. You can show them to Miss Burlison on the train."

"Why, yes, of course. I hope you were not too embarrassed to be my errand boy, John."

He barely heard as he steered her back toward the depot.

"All aboard!" Mad Tom waved an oily rag and got an angry stare from a man dressed as a conductor.

The man went directly to the engineer and began arguing with him. From the tone of the argument, it was good-natured on Tom's part and irritation on the conductor's.

"He usurped the conductor's prerogative," Sarah Jane said.

"Reckon so," Slocum said, not sure what she meant. "You should get your surp on board and tend to Miss Burlison if we're pulling out."

"Why, John, I'm flattered that you noticed I have a lovely 'surp.'" With a swish of her bustle, she went to the lead car, waggled her ass again just for him, and then vanished inside with the boxes.

Slocum climbed up into the cab. Tom worked his levers and the fireman stoked furiously to build a head of steam in the boiler.

"You git Miss Burlison all settled down?"

"She's taking a nap," Slocum said. He hadn't checked to be sure she was aboard, but Sarah Jane would have let him know if her mistress wasn't in the Pullman.

Tom looked at him strangely, shrugged, then tugged on the chain to loose an earsplitting whistle. He leaned out to check the cars as the train began moving. He ducked back, gave more steam to the pistons, and the Yuma Bullet rolled from the yard, hit the switches, and rattled onto the tracks, heading into Texas.

"Never thought we'd get this far," Slocum admitted. He let the air rush past, evaporating the sweat on his face and body. Even the occasional burning cinder didn't keep him from feeling a sense of accomplishment.

"Been a labor of Hercules," Tom said. "Reckon you'll be sad to see it over."

Slocum thought of the money hidden away and how the train sped southward faster than any horse could gallop. The posses were behind him unless a lawman had telegraphed ahead. That seemed less a possibility with every passing minute.

"I should go back and be certain Miss Burlison is all settled down," he said.

"You surely do call it by strange names." Tom laughed, gave another long whistle, and settled down to watch the tracks ahead.

Slocum made his way to the Pullman car, noticing how the Yuma Bullet strained more now because of the extra cars. He opened the door from the platform and ducked inside. Marlene sat on a sofa, needlework in her lap. When she looked over and saw him, her face lit up like the sun coming from behind a cloud.

"How do you like it?"

Slocum had to pull his attention from Marlene to Sarah Jane, who pirouetted about so her skirts flared outward. She wore a red dress with a plunging neckline that any dance hall girl would find daring. With a quick movement, she stopped her spin and faced him. She raised her arms to allow him to fully admire the dress.

"Is that one I brought back for Miss Burlison?"

"Why, uh, yes, it is, John," Sarah Jane said quickly. "She's letting me try it on. I think it is positively stunning, don't you agree?"

Slocum looked at Marlene, who averted her eyes.

"That's mighty generous of you, Miss Burlison, letting your servant try on your duds."

Marlene only nodded.

"I will wear this today and pretend I am attending a grand ball hosted by the crowned heads of Europe," Sarah Jane said, preening in front of the mirror.

Slocum looked past her, out the rear door window. His hand flew to his six-shooter.

"John, what's wrong?" Marlene looked up at his sudden move.

"I saw someone I knew."

"The bounty hunter?" Her voice was barely a whisper audible over the rattle of the wheels against the track.

"Don't expect to see him again," Slocum said in a voice equally low.

"Whatever are you two whispering about?" Sarah Jane came toward them.

Slocum moved fast and turned around, putting his back to the door to protect her if the prospector opened fire. As quietly as he had spoken to Marlene, he said to Sarah Jane, "The prospector's here."

"So he *was* in Deming? He followed you on the morning train?"

"That looks to be so," Slocum said. "I'll see that he doesn't bother us."

"Wait." Sarah Jane clutched his arm. "Can I help?"

Slocum thought about how messy it might be if a gunfight broke out. Walking up to the man and shooting him down didn't appeal to him, and he doubted the prospector would go quietly with a gun shoved in his ribs. Any man who had come this far and dared so much would fight to the death. Whether he had been part of the gang robbing the bank and had double-crossed his partners or had simply seen the gang bury the loot and sought to steal what had already been stolen didn't matter. He had shot it out with Slocum and a posse—or maybe the bank robbers. Determination kept him striving to find his lost gold, and only death would stop him.

Offering a split with him wouldn't work. Finding the gold was an opportunity of a lifetime. Getting half of it would fail to feed the greed driving him.

"Lure him out on the platform between cars. I can take care of him from there."

"Where will you be?"

Slocum considered the matter and realized this wasn't a decent plan. He had nowhere to hide. Then it came to him.

"On the roof of the car. You get him out of the passenger car, and I'll get the drop on him." Slocum knew that wasn't the way it had to be. The instant Sarah Jane charmed him out, he was a dead man. Risking the woman's life was out of the question.

"Give me a couple minutes, then ask him to join you on the platform," Slocum said. As he started for the door, Marlene called out to him.

"John, wait. What are you going to do?"

"Be quiet," snapped Sarah Jane. "This won't take a moment. You tend to your sewing."

Slocum hesitated at the door and looked from the seductress in the red satin dress to the blond girl looking more frightened by the instant.

"She's right, Miss Burlison. We'll be right back. Both of us."

He shot Sarah Jane a hard look, then slipped out the door, found the ladder to the roof, and climbed. The Yuma Bullet rocked from side to side as it took a curve in the tracks, forcing him to drop away from the car. He grabbed frantically as he began to lose traction. The train hit another curve, and he lost his balance entirely. Flat on his belly, sliding toward the edge of the car, he grabbed for anything he could hang on to. A piece of flashing saved him, but he cut his hand. The blood turned his grip slippery.

Flailing about, he finally found purchase on the side of the car, scrambled to the roof, and pushed himself flat there. Hanging on for a moment, he settled down, then slid toward the edge of the roof to look down.

"Damn," he grated out. Sarah Jane already had the prospector out on the platform.

And she had his pants down while she knelt in front of him. The man reached out and put his hands on her head for balance—and this did him in when she lowered her head and threw her shoulder forward into his groin. He yelped, tried to take a step, and got tangled up in his dropped drawers.

He waved his arms around like a windmill and then he fell off the train. The thud as he hit the ground sounded above the clanking wheels. And then the Yuma Bullet highballed on so fast that his moans fell far behind the train.

Sarah Jane stayed on her knees, turned, and looked up over her shoulder. She had a come-hither look on her face and motioned for Slocum to come down and join her.

He wondered if he shouldn't simply let the rocking motion of the train throw him off after the prospector.

18

Slocum gripped the edge of the roof, used the motion of the train, and flipped over to land heavily on the Pullman's platform. Sarah Jane remained on her knees, looking up at him.

"You owe me," she said.

"I would have taken care of him. There was no call for you to push him off the train."

"I rather enjoyed it. He was so easy to get out here, so eager. He must have thought the S&P offered certain services to its passengers." She lifted her hand, fingers wiggling in invitation to Slocum.

"Dressed the way you are, I understand why he believed that."

He reached over, took her hand, and heaved her up. She gave him a sour look as she got her feet under her. She had expected more gallantry on his part. Slocum wondered at how easily she had seduced the prospector and how quick she had been to shove him off the train. For him, getting rid of pursuit was a matter of survival. For her, it was sport, a game, something to amuse her.

"You still owe me," she said, making her way from the passenger car platform to the Pullman's.

She came into his arms and used her lush body to press him against the car wall. His cock responded at once, though whether it was reacting to the movement of the train as it swayed to and fro or the way she rubbed against him like a cat stropping up against a chair leg hardly mattered. Her hand went to his crotch and found what stirred there.

"This is what you owe me, and I want to collect right now."

"Offering him a blow job got you hot?" Slocum didn't try to keep the sarcasm from his voice.

"Yes," she said, hissing like a snake.

Her hand worked down the front of his jeans and began popping open the fly buttons.

"Out here? Like this?"

"No, you're right, John." She gripped hard on his crotch and the bulge there, opened the door, and called out, "Go to the mail car. Give us a half hour." She turned her bright eyes up at Slocum, then corrected, "Make that an hour."

Slocum wasn't too surprised when Marlene obeyed without question. She pointedly looked away as she passed them, pretending not to see how Slocum was corralled. Barely had she left than Sarah Jane kicked shut the door and swarmed all over Slocum, stripping off his coat and dropping his gun belt to the floor.

"Such terrible clothing. I should have bought you something more suitable in Deming."

Slocum watched passively as she pulled back his work shirt and cast it aside, then attacked his jeans with a passion, working them down to expose his groin and the erection growing there. She didn't let him stay out in the air very long. She dived down, her lips circling the tip. She cast a quick look up to see his reaction.

He gasped as she began to apply suction to the very tip of his manhood. His response spurred her on. She took more of him into her mouth, moving down his length inch by inch until he vanished entirely. The rubbery tip bounced off the roof of her mouth and went deeper until she gagged. She backed off and turned her head slightly so the most sensitive parts of his anatomy rubbed against her soft inner cheek. Not content with this, she used her tongue to stroke back and forth on the underside until Slocum felt as if he had turned into a steel bar, unable to get any harder.

"That's about right," she said as she let him pop from her mouth. "Now it's your turn."

He tried to grab behind her head and get her back to keep giving him the intense arousal with her mouth. She twisted to the side and avoided him, rocking back on her heels. Looking down at her, he saw the swell of her breasts billowing up from the plunging neckline. The deep canyon between caught the light and enticed him to reach down and stroke over the bare flesh. Her hands clamped on top of his to keep them pressed hard into her chest. Her breathing turned to deep gasps.

Through the satiny bodice he felt her nipples hardening. He hadn't thought it was possible, but this aroused him even more until his shaft ached with need. Every time his heart beat, his cock jumped. She saw this and moved with a liquid grace, standing. The whole time she rose, she made sure his hands never left her breasts.

"Take me, John. I don't have anything on underneath. Just for you."

She slid her hands down his arms, across his bare flanks, and cupped his buttocks for a moment before lifting her skirts and hooking her bare leg around his. She pulled closer and rubbed herself against him. Wetness boiled from her heated interior and tickled against his manhood.

Slocum reached down and pushed the skirts even higher before running his fingers along the pink canyon between her legs. He got the response he wanted. She moaned and

arched her back to shove herself harder into his probing
fingers. One slid into her and wiggled about. This produced
a cry of pure carnal delight from her.

"I want more, John. That's exciting, but this excites me
more!" She gripped his fleshy shaft and tugged it toward
where his finger slid in and out.

He withdrew his finger, ran his fingernails down her inner
thighs, and opened her even more. Then he spun her about.
She let out a cry and threw out her arms to catch herself on
the back of a plush sofa. With one knee on the cushions,
her hindquarters thrust back into the curve of his groin.

Slocum reached around, caught her waist, and drew her
back slowly. He sank into her from behind, gradually, thrill-
ingly. She tossed her head like a frisky colt when he finally
penetrated her fully.

"Oh, John, you're huge. You fill me up!"

He remained motionless inside her, reveling in the heat
and tightness and how the train's motion caused them to
rock about without expending any effort. The vibration coming up through the Pullman from the wheels gave an added
sensation lacking before. He almost lost control when she
reached back between her legs and caught at his hairy sac to
give it a squeeze.

He got the idea. Pulling away until only the plum-colored
tip of his manhood remained within her, he let the train
taking a gradual curve sway his body. He sank back into
her, the motion matching that of the train.

She put her head down on the back of the sofa and opened
even wider for him. Slocum reached up her body and caught
a dangling tit, squeezing down on it. He groaned at the reaction. Her female sheath tightened all around his buried rod.
Rather than tense up, Slocum abandoned himself to the
train's rolling movement to enter and leave. Vibration and
the motion, her tight wetness, the moans of joy from her
bow-shaped lips, it all worked on him.

He hung suspended for what seemed only an instant

before feeling the white-hot tide rising within him. His balls tightened even more as she stroked over them. He tried to let the train set the pace, but his own desires pushed past any chance for control. He began moving with long, hard thrusts that drove the woman insane with lust. She thrashed about. He held her around the waist, keeping her pulled in deep to the curve of his loins.

Then all chance for rhythm disappeared. He began thrusting with powerful strokes that created friction along his length, and all that mattered was ever deeper penetration. He exploded and spilled his seed and still he kept ramming furiously until he began to melt within her. Finally stepping back when his organ turned limp, he looked at the woman, who remained with her ass up in the air, legs spread, and inviting even more, to no avail. Slocum was completely spent.

She realized no more was forthcoming, dropped her skirts, and turned about to sit on the sofa. Her face was flushed. The blush extended down to the tops of her breasts, which rose and fell heavily.

"That settle accounts?" Slocum asked.

"That makes me want more," she said. "I've never been so—" She abruptly cut off what she meant to say. "You owe me a rematch. When you get in shape again."

Slocum laughed. He had seldom experienced such release. Sleeping for a week to regain his strength was in order.

"I have a fine bed," she said seductively. "It's in that partitioned section behind you."

"It'll take more than that—or anything you can do right now."

"Spoilsport. But later?" The tip of her tongue slipped out and made a slow circuit in wanton invitation.

She pushed down her skirts, stood, and strutted to the back door.

"I'll let you get dressed." She blew him a kiss. With that

she disappeared, leaving Slocum standing naked and alone in the car.

He pulled up his pants and retrieved his shirt from where she had tossed it. He picked up his gun belt as the rear door opened and Marlene rushed in, flustered.

"John, you've got to—oh!" She put her hand over her mouth but kept her gaze fixed on his groin. He still hung out, not having buttoned up again. "I remember that," she said. A small smile flickered, then she sobered quickly. "You and her, you just did—"

"What's wrong?" He settled the cross-draw holster and only then did he tuck himself in and button his fly.

"The mail clerk. The one we picked up in Deming. He's the one who—oh, this is so difficult. He and she were lovers in San Diego and—"

"And Morgan Burlison is sending her to San Antonio to get his daughter away from him."

"That and—" She stared at him. Her hand went to her mouth again as she shook her head. "You know?"

"I figured it out. I was kinda slow but too many things never quite made sense. The two of you switching places would have gone to hell a long time back if I'd listened harder to the way Mad Tom and Jefferson talked around you and Marlene."

The blonde sank to a chair and stared at him. Tears welled in her eyes.

"I didn't want to lie to you, but Marlene thought it would be great fun. She read about it in that book."

"The Mark Twain book?"

She nodded.

"When I got you out of the wrecked car after the bridge collapse, I should have known then. She wanted only to get on to Yuma. Your first thought was of her. She's lucky to have a companion as dedicated." Then Slocum laughed.

"What's so funny?"

"The first time I saw you, I wondered why a lady let her

maid spy on anyone screwing in the next room. She wanted to go there. You didn't have any choice but to accompany her."

"She made me spy, for a little while." Sarah Jane blushed. When she looked up, her expression was bold and challenging. "And I enjoyed it. I wanted to see more, but she insisted on looking instead."

"You wanted to be in there taking part," Slocum said. She blushed again. "What about this mail clerk?"

"I wandered about while you and Marlene were, well, when you were occupied with each other. I saw him in the mail car and could hardly believe my eyes."

"So her pa wants them kept apart."

"Randolph is a bad influence, a very low-life man. But Mr. Burlison is worried about his business rivals kidnapping Marlene to force him to sell the S&P to a new consortium for pennies on the dollar and not go through with a merger he has fashioned with another railroad. That's why he went to San Francisco, to fight off a proxy vote. It's all very complicated, but he doesn't want Marlene used as a threat against him. He certainly doesn't want her around Randolph either."

"Do you think Randolph will harm her?"

"Oh, no, I don't think so," Sarah Jane said, choosing her words carefully. "But he is a wild soul. There's no telling what he might convince her to do."

"She's got an iron will. She won't do anything she doesn't want to," Slocum said.

Then he reconsidered. He had seen women fall in love with outlaws because of the supposed romance. If Morgan Burlison tried too hard to keep his daughter away from someone he considered a bad influence, Marlene would have to show her pa who was right—who was in charge.

"It can be like that," Sarah Jane said, as if reading his mind. "She has an uncontrollable streak that takes a real man to tame."

"Do you know anything about Randolph?"

"I don't like him. I think Mr. Burlison is right and that he's only after Marlene for the family money."

"There's not much they can do aboard the train," Slocum said. "Unless you have other advice, I say let 'em be."

Sarah Jane looked at him. Her eyebrows arched. She started to speak, closed her mouth, and thought for a moment more before saying, "You're asking *me* for advice?"

"You know her—and him—better than I do. I trust your instincts."

Her green eyes fixed on him, as if seeing him in a new light. Slocum got a little uncomfortable until she looked away.

"We'll be stopping at Eagle Pass to take on coal and water," she said. "That's where I'd worry most about her."

"That's a ways down the line," Slocum said. "You have any ideas about how to spend the time it'll take getting there?"

"There's always a card game going in a passenger car. Gin rummy at a penny a point, most likely, though sometimes I see poker games."

"I'm not interested in cards," he said.

She locked eyes with him again.

"I have several of Marlene's books. We can take our pick of titles. She bought several new ones in Deming."

"You want to read to me?"

This caused a tiny smile to dance on the woman's lips.

"You can read, Mr. Slocum. I know it."

"I can read you like an open book." He stepped closer.

She moved until their bodies almost touched.

"I can see we're on the same page."

Slocum was never sure if he kissed Sarah Jane or if she kissed him. It didn't matter since they had found a way to occupy their time all the way to Eagle Pass.

19

"John. John! I can't find her!"

Slocum forced one eyelid up. It took him a second to focus on Sarah Jane's lovely face. He pushed up to one elbow in the narrow bed and tried to make out what bothered her so. Then it hit him. He swung out of bed, his feet hitting the Pullman car floor so hard an echo ran from one end to the other.

"We're not moving," he said, pulling on his jeans. The heavy blue work shirt got buttoned down fast, and he had his boots on before he strapped the six-shooter to his hip. "Where'd she go?"

"We pulled into Eagle Pass a half hour ago. You were sleeping so soundly I didn't have the heart to wake you." She smiled shyly. "If you were half as worn out as I was, you deserved the rest." Then the smile vanished. "I went back to the mail car, thinking Marlene would be with Randolph. They were both gone."

Slocum got to his feet, started forward, stopped, went back, and kissed Sarah Jane soundly.

"It's not your fault. It's mine for not bird-dogging her

181

after you warned me about the mail clerk." He rushed forward, swung out, and made his way along the side of the tender.

Mad Tom cursed as he worked on a steam valve. He never looked up as he said, "You better bring me some damned good news, Slocum, or I'll throw you off the train. This here valve's broke, and I can't fix the mother-lovin' son of a bitch."

"How long before the Bullet's ready to roll?"

"We're only a hunnerd miles outta San Antonio and the valve has to go bust." Tom looked up. "I'll push the damned Yuma Bullet all the way into San Antonio if I have to. We'll be there in three hours. Less, once we highball on outta here."

"Take your time," Slocum said.

Tom swore so sulfurously that Slocum stared at him.

"She done run off, didn't she?" Tom asked.

"With the mail clerk."

"That puny sprout? Of course she'd run off with somebody like that 'cuz she can wrap him around her little finger." Tom stared hard at Slocum. "Not that she could ever do a thing like that to *you*."

Slocum accepted the jibe without comment. He had been duped and hadn't twigged to the real situation until close to when Sarah Jane had fessed up. The way Marlene—the real Marlene—acted since Deming had caused him to begin wondering about their switched identities. From what Sarah Jane explained, the Mark Twain book caused Marlene to think this was possible and ever so naughty.

"Don't go without us," Slocum said, jumping to the ground.

"I oughta quit, that's what I oughta do." The engineer returned to his repairs, working himself up into even grander obscenities.

Slocum walked to the mail car. The door had been pushed open and the clerk was nowhere to be seen. He waved to a railroad bull. The man came over, tapping a slungshot against his left palm, as if wondering about Slocum's right to be here.

"The clerk's lit out," Slocum said. "You see where he went?"

"Don't know if I should even talk to you. The boss's daughter said somebody'd be askin' after her—and him."

"Morgan Burlison hired me to be her bodyguard. Randolph has kidnapped her."

"Didn't look like that to me. She and him was all lovey-dovey when they went . . ." He turned and looked in the direction of the road leading from the depot down Eagle Pass's main street.

Slocum ran out, inquired of the station agent, and got a similar reply. Marlene had convinced everyone that he was out to do her wrong. Disgusted, Slocum considered fetching the silver and gold coins he had hidden away and letting Marlene and her beau go off together. But he couldn't do that. Burlison had hired him to safeguard his daughter, even if Slocum had been confused as to her identity much of the way from San Diego. Even taking how he had been duped into account, he had protected her well.

Sarah Jane, too.

He started down the street, considering where the couple would go. He went into the hotel. The clerk was snoring behind the counter and didn't take kindly when Slocum woke him.

"Did a dark-haired woman with a young man register here within the last hour or so?"

"Nope, nobody like that. Was she good looking?" Seeing Slocum's expression, the clerk shrugged. "I woulda noticed."

Slocum left without a word, then froze on the hotel's front steps. He stared in disbelief as a man hobbled down the center of the main street. How Big Joe Joseph had gotten this far was a wonderment. His leg was all busted up and he used a crutch made from a cottonwood branch. His face had met the wrong side of a prickly pear pad, and his buckskins hung in tatters from his gaunt body. If Slocum had been through hell, Big Joe had come the same way crawling on his belly.

Ducking back into the hotel lobby, Slocum ran through to the rear exit. He came out in an alley not far from the livery stables. If Marlene and her boyfriend weren't in a hotel room, buying horses to cut across Texas or maybe go into Mexico made sense. As Slocum approached the stables, he spotted Randolph with two men, both well dressed. They were arguing. Taking advantage, Slocum went to the front of the stables, where Marlene paced anxiously. He was within a few feet of her when she noticed him. Before she could cry out, he clamped his hand over her mouth, winced as her teeth sank into his flesh, then bodily picked her up and carried her inside.

"Quit fighting me," Slocum said. "Your pa hired me to get you to San Antonio all safe and sound, and I'm going to do just that. You can run off with Randolph then, but not before I deliver you to your ma."

"Papa would never let me go with Randolph. Ever!"

Slocum cocked his head to one side as the argument between Randolph and the men intensified. He caught enough now to once more put his hand over the girl's mouth and bodily carry her to an open window at the rear of the livery. Everything the men outside said rang loud and clear.

She fought and tried to scream, then her struggles subsided. Slocum took the chance of putting her down. Marlene's face turned bright red with anger, and before she could blurt out anything, he silenced her again.

"Your swain just bartered you to those men for one hundred dollars."

"The one in the gray suit's Papa's enemy. Kent Gallardo. He's been trying to force Papa to vote to sell the S&P for months. He . . . he *bought* me?"

"More like Randolph sold you," Slocum said.

"But he said he loved me."

"He loves money more, and he didn't bargain very hard to get more than a hundred dollars for you. If Gallardo ransoms you for your pa's vote, something tells me your family's going to be dirt poor."

"Randolph said—"

"I'll take care of them for you," Slocum said, "if you'll do me a favor."

"I want to rip his eyes out! I'll feed his entrails to the buzzards. I . . . I'll tie him to the tracks so the Yuma Bullet runs over him!"

"Your pa hired me to do all that," Slocum said. "All I want is for you to tell a man I've crossed the border, and last you saw of me, I was heading into Mexico. Tell him I'm traveling with Randolph and make up any story you choose as to why you want me dead."

"All right. You can shoot him down for me. Or whatever you're planning. It sounds awful."

"Painful," Slocum said. "He'll suffer in ways you don't want to know about."

"Who do I tell this to?"

"His name's Big Joe and he won't be hard to find," Slocum said. Slocum quickly described the bounty hunter.

"She hasn't said a word all the way from Eagle Pass," Sarah Jane said. "What did you do to her there?"

"Nothing much. We traded favors."

Sarah Jane looked at him curiously.

"Let's say a problem of mine is hunting down a problem of hers in Mexico."

"I don't understand."

Slocum smiled and shook his head. Offering to tar and feather Randolph had been the easy part, especially after he winged Gallardo's bodyguard and chased the railroad magnate off amid a hail of bullets. A broad suggestion that Randolph might escape both tar and feathers and painful torture had set him on the trail for Mexico. After Marlene had told the bounty hunter that Slocum and Randolph were hightailing it into the interior to hide with the Yaqui Indians, he had taken off right away. Slocum reckoned he would overtake Randolph in a day or so. What happened then fired his imagination.

The train whistle sounded three long blasts as the Yuma Bullet pulled into the San Antonio station.

"That's her, Mrs. Burlison," Sarah Jane said. "She's a lovely woman."

"I see where Marlene gets her looks."

Sarah Jane shot him an angry look, but it faded when he pulled her close and gave her a small kiss on the back of the neck. She wiggled her butt against his crotch, which was meant as an invitation, just as Mad Tom applied the brakes and sent them both staggering a step or two.

"Miss Burlison, I'll get your bags," Sarah Jane called.

"Go to hell. You can both go to hell, where you deserve each other!" Marlene flounced off after giving Slocum a particularly black look.

She went out onto the platform and allowed her mother to hug her. They went off together to a carriage waiting in front of the station.

Slocum and Sarah Jane exited and stood silently, looking around until a well-dressed man came up.

"Mr. Slocum? I am Bertram Tunney, Mr. Burlison's San Antonio manager. He instructed me to give this to you." Tunney reached into his inner coat pocket and withdrew a bulging envelope.

"I'd hoped for gold, but scrip will do," Slocum said. Tunney shrugged and walked away to a buggy of his own.

"What are you going to do now, John?"

"Give this to you. You earned it." He handed her the envelope. "There ought to be three hundred dollars there."

"I can't take this. It's your money."

"After what happened with Randolph, do you think Marlene is going to keep you on? She has to blame someone, and blaming me isn't going to be enough for her. Take the money."

"Very well, John, but what are you going to do?"

"Ride north." He waited for her to say something more, but she looked down shyly. He put his index finger under her chin and raised her face. Again he wasn't sure who started the kiss. They were both breathless when they broke apart.

"I'll miss you, John."

"Find something worth doing," Slocum said. "Being Marlene's maid isn't a fit job."

"But I—"

Slocum turned as tears welled up in her soft green eyes. He hopped down from the platform, went to the engine, and saw that both Mad Tom and the fireman were gone. It took him a few minutes to unfasten the metal plate and fish out the three sacks of gold and silver he had hidden there. He opened one sack and pulled out ten of the twenty-dollar gold pieces and left them on Tom's drop seat. Then he left the rail yard and found a stable willing to sell him a good horse, gear, and supplies adequate to get him a couple weeks into the belly of Texas.

It was twilight when he left San Antonio behind, and the moon was rising as he made camp and prepared some grub. He was just finishing his meal when he heard the sound of an approaching horse. Looking up, he saw Sarah Jane decked out in trail clothes, astride a smallish mare.

"What?" she asked. "You didn't think I could ride?"

"I knew you could," he said. "I didn't know you could track."

"I smelled that coffee halfway to San Antonio. Are you going to offer me some?"

Slocum held up his tin cup, willing to give her a lot more than a cup of boiled coffee. He could even tell her about the gold. Later.

Watch for

SLOCUM AND THE REBEL CANYON RAIDERS

423rd novel in the exciting SLOCUM series
from Jove

Coming in May!